"You can't deny that was a kiss for the ages."

"I don't deny it. At all." The flood of warmth in her body that came from thinking about the kiss only made her angry. *And you threw it all away.*

"I still think about it sometimes."

Sophie narrowed her sights on him. Was that an actual blush of pink on his cheeks? "You do?"

"Well, sure." Jake took another drink and leaned forward, placing the glass on the coffee table. When he sat back, his hand brushed hers, which was planted on the sofa between them. He pulled his away, leaving her nothing but painfully aware of his effect on her. An instant of touching and he'd stoked the fire inside her, the one that had always burned brightest for him. "Don't you?"

Of course she did. How could he be so clueless about what it had meant to her? She still thought about that kiss...and everything that had come after it.

* * *

A Christmas Temptation is part of the Eden Empire series from Karen Booth.

Dear Reader,

Thanks for picking up *A Christmas Temptation*! It's the first Eden Empire book about the heiresses of the Eden family, who are about to inherit their grandmother's Manhattan department store.

Sophie is the youngest Eden heiress, still mourning the death of her grandmother and determined to make the store a grand success again. She's not focused on the multibillion-dollar value of her inheritance. She's all about family tradition. Her sister, Mindy, has her own thriving business and wants no part of Eden's. She wants to sell.

Enter Jake Wheeler, Sophie's unrequited love. He's sexy and smooth and determined to leverage their friendship into a deal. Little does he know just how deep Sophie is determined to dig in her heels. I love the friction between these two, further amped up by Sophie's love of Christmas and Jake's hatred of it. When Sophie drags the reason why out of him, it breaks her heart. Fixing Christmas is just as big a part of this story as finding their way to love.

I hope you enjoy this story of unrequited love fulfilled! Drop me a line anytime at karen@karenbooth.net. I love hearing from readers!

Karen

KAREN BOOTH

A CHRISTMAS TEMPTATION

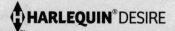

Recycling programs
for this product may
not exist in your area.

ISBN-13: 978-1-335-97188-3

A Christmas Temptation

Copyright © 2018 by Karen Booth

All rights reserved. Except for use in any review, the reproduction or
utilization of this work in whole or in part in any form by any electronic,
mechanical or other means, now known or hereafter invented, including
xerography, photocopying and recording, or in any information storage
or retrieval system, is forbidden without the written permission of the
publisher, Harlequin Enterprises Limited, 22 Adelaide St. West, 40th Floor,
Toronto, ON M5H 4E3, Canada.

This is a work of fiction. Names, characters, places and incidents are
either the product of the author's imagination or are used fictitiously,
and any resemblance to actual persons, living or dead, business
establishments, events or locales is entirely coincidental.

This edition published by arrangement with Harlequin Books S.A.

For questions and comments about the quality of this book,
please contact us at CustomerService@Harlequin.com.

® and TM are trademarks of Harlequin Enterprises Limited or its
corporate affiliates. Trademarks indicated with ® are registered in the
United States Patent and Trademark Office, the Canadian Intellectual
Property Office and in other countries.

Printed in U.S.A.

Karen Booth is a Midwestern girl transplanted in the South, raised on '80s music, Judy Blume and the films of John Hughes. When she takes a break from the art of romance, she's listening to music with her nearly grown kids or sweet-talking her husband into making her a cocktail. Learn more about Karen at karenbooth.net.

Books by Karen Booth

Harlequin Desire

The Best Man's Baby
The Ten-Day Baby Takeover
Snowed in with a Billionaire

The Eden Empire

A Christmas Temptation

Visit her Author Profile page at Harlequin.com, or karenbooth.net, for more titles.

For Melissa Jeglinski,
my amazing agent and friend.
I'm so thankful to have you on my side!

One

Eden's Department Store offered a dazzling array of merchandise, but in Sophie Eden's mind, everything started with the shoes. Thus, she always began her workday in the shoe department, surveying the latest and chitchatting with the salespeople as they prepared for the day's shoppers. Sophie often devoted ten or fifteen minutes to the pursuit before heading upstairs to her office. Some days she'd even try on something new. Not today. With less than a month until Christmas, and the vultures circling, getting right to work was the most pressing matter.

She bustled through the department down the wide center promenade, past the Lucite and chrome displays of sling-backs and stilettos, beneath the splendid crystal chandeliers that dotted the high coffered ceiling. Her delicate heels click-clacked on the gleaming white marble floor. Her shoes were particularly magnificent today—Manolo Blahnik pumps with a slim leather tie at the ankle, in Christmas red. The color choice was no coincidence. The holidays were Sophie's favorite time of year, and she was going to sneak in every second of cheer she could. She already knew Christmas would be difficult this year. This would be the first without Gram, her grandmother, the founder of Eden's.

Sophie rounded a turn as the aisle spoked off to the various sections of the department known to fashion editors all over the world as "shoe heaven." Tucked back in the far corner was the vestibule with the private elevator that would take her upstairs to the true guts of the Eden's operation. She sucked in a deep, cleansing breath as she took her short ride up one floor. Normally, she loved her job, but right now it was much farther from heaven than the number on the elevator door suggested.

"Good morning, Lizzie," Sophie said, greeting her assistant. She shrugged off her cream-colored wool coat and slung it over her arm. Considering the dirt and grime of the city, such a light color was a stupid idea, but Sophie loved the way it showed off her red hair. It was one of her best assets.

Lizzie popped up from behind her desk, all sunshine and raw energy. Her platinum pixie cut was extra spiky today. "Good morning, Ms. Eden. How are you?"

"Depends. How's my day looking?"

"You've already received three gift baskets from real-estate developers this morning."

"It's barely nine o'clock."

"The couriers start delivering at eight."

Sophie shook her head. This had been the drill for the last month, ever since her grandmother, Victoria Eden, had passed away. Everyone knew that Sophie and her sister, Mindy, would inherit Eden's. Their grandmother spoke of it often, at runway shows and cocktail parties and even to the press. Eden's was a business built for women, by women, and it would be run by women for as long as Victoria Eden could see it through.

The will was to be read the week before Christmas when the heirs could gather. It was viewed as a formality, though. Sophie and her sister, Mindy, would own the store. Thus the influx of gift baskets, flowers, phone calls and emails. It wasn't that anyone was particularly interested in Eden's as a business. They were after the building and the land. Everyone assumed Sophie and Mindy would want to sell. Mindy was desperate to do so. Sophie was diametrically opposed to the idea.

"Oh, and your sister called to say she will not be able to come by today after all," Lizzie said as she trailed Sophie into her office.

"Lovely." Sophie made no effort to disguise the unhappiness in her voice. She and Mindy were at odds right now. "I'll have to give her a call and see what her problem is." She got settled in her chair, which was custom upholstered in peacock blue velvet with gold nail-head trim. She pulled her laptop from her bag and set it on her sleek white glass-topped desk. "Anything else?"

"Everything's in your calendar. You have a meeting with the department heads at two this afternoon. Also, Reginald will be up to do the holiday decorations in your office soon. I tried to get him to come earlier in the morning, but it just wasn't possible. I think they're all still recovering from installing the holiday window displays."

Sophie waved it off. "Yes. Of course. My office is definitely the bottom of the priority list. And I'm glad they're coming while I'm here. I'd like to be able to pitch in." Sophie loved decorating for Christmas. It was one of her absolute favorite pursuits.

"Do you think Reginald will actually let you help? You know how he is." Lizzie bugged her eyes and whispered, "Control freak."

"And I'm about to be the president of Eden's Department Store. Plus, he loved Gram, and he knows how close we were." Sophie wasn't sure who had cried harder at her grandmother's funeral—her or Reginald. "I'm sure he'll be nothing but accommodating."

Lizzie made her way to the door but stopped before exiting. "Oh. I almost forgot. Jake Wheeler called again last night. Also, he sent the fruit." Lizzie pointed to the credenza behind Sophie's desk. Three elaborate cellophane-wrapped baskets sat atop it.

Jake Wheeler. How could one man's name send both a flash of anger and a flutter of delight through her body at the same time?

"Did he leave a message?"

"He did. He wanted me to remind you that it's very important he speaks to you."

"Of course he did. He's a man accustomed to getting everything he wants." Sophie picked up the fruit basket. "Put this in the employee lounge. Someone should enjoy it."

Lizzie held out her arms, which dropped a bit under the weight of the basket. "Don't you want to read the card first?"

Sophie didn't really want to read the card, but knowledge was king and she needed to know what Jake Wheeler was thinking. Otherwise, he was a mystery. He always had been.

Sophie grabbed the gold-trimmed envelope and ripped it from the plastic. "Thank you, Lizzie."

"Of course, Ms. Eden. You know where to find me if you need anything."

Sophie sat in her chair, her back straight and chin held high as she slid a manicured finger under the envelope flap. There was no telling what Jake had written on this card. When they were in business school together, everything out of his mouth was witty and warm. It was one of the things that first drew her to him. That and his unforgettable green eyes.

Dear Sophie,
  You can't ignore my phone calls forever.
Sooner or later, I'll get through to you.
Best,
Jake

A zip of electricity ran along Sophie's spine. From somewhere deep in the recesses of her mind, the sound of Jake's sexy rumble of a voice had been set free. It was like a wild animal, pouncing on her. She'd forgotten the way it made her feel. A wave of warmth started in her chest and rolled back over her shoulders. She reclined in her chair and closed her eyes, recalling the magical moment when he'd first kissed her eight years ago, his insistent lips bringing every fantasy she'd had about him to life. He'd kissed her like he meant it, his arms tight around her waist, pulling her body into his. It was a dream come true in so many ways. She'd spent two years desperate for him to do that, trying so hard to be the kind of woman who would catch his eye. Finally, she'd done it.

Little had she known Jake Wheeler would break her heart and shatter her opinion of him in less than twenty-four hours.

Sophie's eyes flew open when there was a knock at her door.

Lizzie stood before her, plainly concerned. It was not like Sophie to sit at her desk with her eyes closed. "Ms. Eden? Reginald is here."

Sophie bolted upright and scrambled out from behind her desk. "Yes. Great. Good morning, Reginald. Please, come right in."

"Everything okay?" Lizzie asked under her breath.

"Just a slight headache."

"Good morning, Ms. Eden." Reginald, Eden's creative director, floated into her office and began surveying the walls and windows. "We're here to transform your office into a glamorous winter wonderland." Reginald was a bald, spindly man with thick horn-rimmed glasses who always wore a suit with a bow tie. His ensemble today was navy blue with a lavender pinstripe, the tie matching the stripes. Reginald did not do quiet, dull or subtle—precisely the reason Eden's window displays were one of the most popular Christmas attractions in the city.

Two young women rushed in behind him, lugging large boxes overflowing with sparkly silver and white garland. They set down their armfuls in the corner of Sophie's office and hurried back out into the hall, presumably for more supplies.

"What's the plan?" Sophie asked, filled with a mix of anticipation and sadness. Decorating one's office was Gram's tradition. She wanted Christmas oozing from every corner of Eden's. It helped to make the most arduous month of the year tolerable.

Reginald cast a doubtful look down at her, his glasses sliding to the tip of his nose. "You aren't planning on staying, are you? I work best unencumbered. And unsupervised."

Sophie frowned. "You used to let Gram help you when you decorated her office."

"That was different. She was the matriarch of the store. A queen. An unparalleled woman."

Sophie didn't need any more of this speech. She was well aware of the grand specter of her grandmother. She lived and worked under it every day. Sophie, along with her sister, would eventually fill the matriarchal role, but it wasn't right to claim it now. That was a position that must be earned, not inherited. "Got it."

Reginald patted her on the shoulder. "Trust me. It'll be stunning when you return." He made a grand gesture for the door. "Now shoo."

Sophie grabbed her cell phone from her desk and stepped out into the hall. Gram's office was right next to hers. The door was still open, and Sophie flipped on the light. It still looked so strange with no Gram. Sophie had no trouble sketching in what was missing—her grandmother, with her trademark strawberry blond bob with thick bangs, never a hair out of place. On a day like today, Sophie could imagine her in a tailored dress in a fun color, perhaps a bold floral, accessorized with gold bangles and diamond earrings. She was always glamorous perfection.

Gram's office was a similarly colorful and pristine place, with everything exactly as it was on the last day she'd worked, at the end of October. Sophie had a lot of regrets about the last time she'd seen Gram. Sophie's day had been horrible and she'd only waved goodbye to her grandmother when she left the office. If she'd known Gram would have a heart attack in her sleep that night, she would have taken one last time to say *I love you*. She would have run out from behind her desk, grabbed her and given her one last hug.

Sophie turned off the light. She wasn't ready to use Gram's office. She might never be. It would only make her feel sad and inadequate. She could just imagine the looks on people's faces when they walked into the room and realized that the woman sitting behind the desk did not possess the gravitas of her predecessor.

Instead, Sophie ducked into an empty cubicle hidden behind the reception area. She dialed the number for her sister, Mindy, who answered right away.

"Lizzie said you aren't coming in today. Why not?" Sophie asked.

"Because it's December and one of our high-production printers is broken and my team is struggling to fill orders. I don't have time to spend at Eden's." Mindy had her own successful business, By Min-vitation Only, an online shop that sold high-end custom cards and invitations. "Everyone needs their Christmas cards yesterday. It's a madhouse over here."

"Oh. Okay. I understand."

"Don't sound so disappointed, Soph. You knew this was going to happen. You knew I couldn't simply drop everything and take on new responsibilities. I appreciate that you're steering the ship at Eden's until Gram's will is read, but I need you to accept the reality of our situation."

"And what is that exactly?" Sophie crossed her legs and bobbed her foot, stealing a glimpse of her red pumps. God, she loved those shoes. Mr. Blahnik was a genius.

"Today is our reality. I am too busy to play a role in the store. Today I'm dealing with Christmas, but after that is New Year's and Valentine's Day. There is no downtime for me. I've worked hard to build my business, and I'm not stepping away from it."

Sophie understood her sister's predicament and her argument. She did. She just wished it wasn't the case. Now that Gram wasn't around to offer advice and solve problems, Sophie was perpetually out of her depth. And alone.

"Eden's is a lost cause, Soph. You'll be much happier when you just admit it," Mindy said.

"It is not. Gram didn't think so, and I don't think so, either. We can turn it around. Our earnings were up two percent last quarter."

"And my earnings were up twenty."

Way to rub it in my face. "I get it, Mindy. But this is our family business."

"I'm family. And I have a business. I'm telling you, as soon as the will is read, you and I need to sell Eden's to the highest bidder, pocket the cash, and then you need to come work for me. Easy peasy. We'll both have it made."

Mindy made it sound so simple and obvious, but she hadn't made promises to their grandmother. She hadn't spent the last three years working for Gram, learning and growing and soaking up every drop she could of her genius. "I'm not prepared to talk about anything until after Christmas. It's in poor taste."

Sophie stepped out of the cubicle and tiptoed over to her office door to sneak a peek through the tiny gap between the door and the jamb.

Reginald rushed right over. "Oh, no you don't." He quickly closed the door, right in her face.

"Fine," Mindy said, sounding impatient. "But will you at least call Jake Wheeler and listen to his pitch? The man is ridiculously persistent. He's calling me twice a day."

There it was—that name again. "I know. He sent me a fruit basket."

"He's got superdeep pockets, Sophie. And he sure speaks fondly of you. You'd think you two were exes the way he talks about you."

Sophie leaned back against the wall, her vision narrowing just as her lips pinched together. "You know that's not the case."

"Oh, I know. I know the whole story. He's the one who got away."

Sophie shook her head. "He is not. He's the snake who slithered away. And I hardly had him to begin with." *Just one unbelievably hot night of abandon.*

"Regardless. Call him."

"I'll think about it." Sophie already knew there was no way she would call Jake. There was a lot of wisdom in the adage about not clawing at old wounds. He'd hurt her. Badly. She would never, ever forgive him.

"Think harder. I'd like to cross him off my to-do list."

Sophie stifled a snort. Jake Wheeler had spent two years on her "to-do" list.

Years later, she still regretted it like crazy.

Granted, expressing condolences was not Jake Wheeler's strongpoint. He'd found it much easier to get through life by glossing over sad moments and enjoying pleasant ones. But after three unreturned phone calls, a sympathy card that garnered no response and an ignored charity donation in her grandmother's name, he was certain Sophie Eden was not impressed with his efforts.

Jake's admin, Audrey, buzzed the line in his office. "Ms. Eden's assistant is on the line, Mr. Wheeler."

Jake picked up his phone. "Lizzie, I'm worried that if we continue to spend this much time on the phone, people will start to get the wrong impression of our working relationship."

"Sir? You remembered my name?"

"How could I not? Is this our fourth or fifth time speaking?"

"I'm not sure, sir. Probably the fifth."

"And I'm guessing you know why I'm calling." Jake rocked forward and back in his chair, watching out the window of his tenth-floor office in the luxury steel-and-glass tower of 7 Bryant Park. He had stunning views of the New York Public Library and other midtown Manhattan landmarks, but the one he enjoyed most was that of the building's namesake. Down on the street, a temporary Christmas market was set up with vendors, music and ice skating. The holiday disruption had been overtaking the normally peaceful green space every December in recent years. Jake couldn't wait for January, when it would all be gone.

"I do. And I'm very sorry, but Ms. Eden is not available right now."

"Can you at least tell me when she'll be back in the office?"

"She's here all the time, Mr. Wheeler. But her schedule is packed and always changing, as I'm sure you can understand. It's December. She runs one of the largest department stores in Manhattan. It's a very busy time."

"Of course." Jake tapped his pen on his desk. "Did she get the fruit basket I sent?"

"She did. And she was generous enough to share it with the staff. Everyone has enjoyed it greatly. Thank you."

Jake wasn't sure what more he could do to get her to return his phone calls, and he certainly couldn't arrive at a conclusion about why she was avoiding him. Their last interaction, years ago, at business school graduation, had been nothing but pleasant and cordial. They'd both agreed to let their shared history remain where it belonged—in the past.

"But she's not there right now?" He purposely added a heavy tone of suspicion to the question. It was the end of the workday. If Sophie was too busy to pick up the phone, she had to still be at the office.

"I'm sorry, but she's not available right now. No."

Jake wasn't sure what that meant, but he knew he was getting the runaround. "Fine. I'd like to leave a message. Again. My name is Jake Wheeler, and my number is—"

"Ms. Eden has your number."

Jake choked back a frustrated grumble. "Please remind her that it's very important. I need to speak to her."

"She knows, sir. I've delivered each one of your messages personally." Judging by the tone in her voice, Sophie's assistant was losing her patience. That much they had in common.

"Great. Thank you." Jake hung up the phone, more frustrated now than ever. He had to get Sophie to talk to him. He had to meet with her. Jake was a member of an exclusive investment group called the War Chest. It was run by financier Jacob Lin, and they tackled only the biggest of big deals—ones that required several sets of deep pockets. Jake had suggested Eden's when Sophie's grandmother had died. The other War Chest members, hoteliers Sawyer and Noah Locke and real-estate broker Michael Kelly, along with Jacob, had all voted yes on the idea. Jake assured them with a great deal of confidence that he had an inside track with Sophie. Of course, until a month ago, he'd thought he did have an inside track. He and Sophie were best friends in business school. For a brief but memorable twenty-four hours, they'd been more.

"Audrey?" he called out into the void of his office.

In seconds flat, Jake's assistant snapped to attention in his office doorway. Audrey was fastidious, hyperorganized and very opinionated. "Sir, I really think it's too late for coffee. You'll get edgy, and caffeine is disruptive to sleep patterns."

"I don't need coffee. I'm wondering if you have any ideas on convincing a woman to call you back."

"Jewelry. Flowers. Chocolate. A profession of love."

Jake shook his head. "Not like that. I know *that*. I mean, in a professional setting."

"So nothing romantic?"

Jake didn't have to think about that one. He and Sophie were better off sticking to business. Of that much, he was sure. "Not intentionally romantic, but Ms. Eden does appreciate the finer things in life if that helps."

Audrey nodded. "Ah, yes. Your unromantic fruit-basket recipient."

"Precisely."

"And that didn't go over well? Who doesn't love a fruit basket?"

"I have no idea."

"Flowers?"

"Isn't that a cliché?"

"Not if you buy a ridiculous amount of her favorites and show up with them in person."

Jake raised both eyebrows at his assistant.

"That's what my husband did when he proposed."

"I'm not proposing marriage."

"But you are trying to talk a woman into selling

her business when it's been only a few weeks since the family matriarch passed away. You might want to go big."

"Excellent point."

"Any idea what her favorite flower is?"

Jake had a recollection of a dinner at a professor's house and Sophie commenting about the centerpiece. "The ones that look like roses, but aren't actually roses. I think it starts with a *p*."

"Peonies?"

"Yes. That's it. Pink would be good."

"I'm on it."

"Thanks, Audrey." Jake sat back in his chair and turned his sights to the city again. The sky was dark, snow flurries starting to fall. Could it be as simple as flowers? Jake doubted it highly. Nothing was ever simple with Sophie. But he needed to mix things up or he would lose ground. He knew for a fact that other investors and developers were courting her and her sister. His pitch would work so much better in person, especially if he could get Sophie alone. She'd always dropped the tougher parts of her veneer when it was just the two of them.

Visions of Sophie flashed in his head—her lush red hair, her full lips, the way her brown eyes flickered with gold when she smiled. Each thought of her was more beautiful than the last. They'd been drawn to each other from the moment they met at a business school mixer. She laughed at his jokes and flirted like crazy with him, touching his arm and flashing her gorgeous eyes. They shared an immediate chemistry that was off the charts. In any other scenario, Jake would have taken her home that very first night.

But he made a point of keeping their relationship platonic, even when there had been days where that required superhuman strength. He wanted her. There was no question about that. But he knew how brutal those two years of school were going to be. He couldn't afford to have a fellow classmate royally pissed at him for seducing her and then calling things off before they got serious, which was what Jake did every time. The panic when a woman started to get close to him was real. There was no erasing the part of his history that made him feel that way.

Still, the night they both gave in to their attraction had been magical. He couldn't deny that. Two years of waiting and wondering and resisting can make giving in that much more delicious. They'd been studying at the library for hours, preparing for one of their final exams. Exhausted, Jake had asked Sophie if she wanted to go get a beer. She then realized how late it was, and in a panic asked Jake back to her apartment.

"My roommate is out of town and I'm supposed to feed her cat. The poor thing is probably starving. Come to my place. Okay?"

"Yeah. Sure. I just can't study anymore."

When they got to Sophie's, after the cat had been fed, they sat on the couch and had a drink. To this day, he could remember the moment when he'd decided to finally kiss her. She'd put her gorgeous red hair in a pile on top of her head, and she'd laughed at one of his goofy jokes, quite possibly a little too hard, and her hair slumped to the side. She'd pulled at the tie, and it tumbled down onto her shoulders. Maybe he'd been tired. Maybe it was the beer. He only knew that after nearly two years of waiting, he had to kiss her.

So he did.

No woman had melted into him the way Sophie did. Her lips were pillow soft, her sweet smell truly beguiling, and her hands were everywhere. Before he knew what was happening, she was tugging his shirt up over his head and pushing him down on the couch, her body settling between his legs and driving him crazy with desire.

The moment when she sat back up, took his hand and led him to her bedroom was one of the most surreal. He'd fantasized about Sophie plenty, but she was also one of the only female friendships he'd managed to not only build, but maintain. He'd thought about it for a second that night, considered telling her it wasn't a good idea for them to go to bed together, but once she took off her top and her stunning red hair tumbled back onto her shoulders? He was a goner.

They'd made love three times that night. They even took a shower together in the morning, which should have been enough to convince him that Sophie might be the one worth trying for more with. But when the time came for him to think about going back to his place, and it was clear that there were expectations for the two of them to discuss where this next went, Jake panicked just as he always had.

"You know, Sophie, last night was amazing, and I will always remember it. But we're such great friends and we both have so much we want to do in our careers. I think it's best if we chalk this up to two friends blowing off a little steam together."

He knew the instant he'd said it that she deserved better. Sophie had wrapped her robe around her tight and nodded, forcing a smile. "Oh, yeah. Of course. A couple of friends hooking up, right? Happens all the time."

He'd heard the hurt in her voice, but he told himself that with time it would go away. Sophie was too special—too smart, too funny, too beautiful. Some amazing guy, somewhere, would meet her and snatch her up and treat her the way she deserved to be treated. Jake wasn't that guy. He didn't possess the trust to let someone in like that. He'd tried and failed. He was self-aware enough to understand this particular shortcoming.

After their one night together, his friendship with Sophie quickly returned to its previous state, or at least close to it. Neither of them mentioned what had happened, they helped each other study, and soon enough, it was time to graduate. They'd hugged for a very long time that day. They'd wished each other luck. It was all perfectly normal and uncontroversial, except for Sophie's parting words.

"I love you, Jake."

Stunned, he ignored what she'd said and simply let her walk away. A few times during the eight years since then, Sophie's words had resurfaced in his memory. He always fought them back. *I love you* was something a woman said right before she left forever. And sure enough, that was exactly what Sophie Eden did.

Two

Once again, Sophie had to start her workday by rushing through the shoe department, but she didn't make it far before she stopped dead in her tracks. A stunning pair of chartreuse-green Blahniks had appeared since yesterday. Perched on a tall pedestal, with small bundles of sparkly beads and intricate lacing up the front, they were like a phoenix rising from the ashes of the other, lesser shoes. They stole her breath. She had to have them. They were sexy as all get-out. If only she had a man to test them out on. Her dating calendar had been tragically light since coming to work at Eden's.

"Marie," Sophie called out to the department head. She was training a new salesperson. "Can you set aside a pair of these for me?"

Marie smiled generously. "I thought those might catch your eye. They're already in your office, sitting on your desk. Just have Lizzie buzz me if you don't like them and I'll have someone come by to pick them up."

"Do you really think I might not like them?"

Marie shook her head. "Not a chance."

Sophie grinned. Her job was sometimes overwhelming, but this was one of her favorite perks. Without another second to waste, she rushed back to the elevator and up to the top floor.

"Morning, Lizzie. What's the gift-basket count today?"

"Five, I'm afraid. I think people are trying to outdo each other now."

Sophie trailed into her office and set down her things, bypassing the baskets and zeroing in on the beautiful heels nestled in a box and tissue on her desk. She sat down and removed her pumps and worked her feet into the new shoes. "Did we at least get anything good?"

"How do two dozen gourmet caramel apples slathered in chocolate and sprinkles sound?"

"Like I need to skip lunch. Which is perfect because today is crazy." Sophie stood up and took the new pumps for a spin around her office. "What do you think?"

"Honestly? Sexy. Super sexy."

Sophie admired her feet again. Sure her toes were pinched and her arches would be screaming by the time the day was over, but she didn't care. Right now, beautiful shoes were the only things that were making her happy. "If Marie comes by, tell her I'm keeping them."

"Will do. Now, back to your crazy day. There's a long list of fires that need putting out all over the store."

"Great. Can't wait." Sophie gave the statement all the sarcasm it deserved.

"All six employees of the coat check have come down with the flu. We got someone from housewares to fill in, but you know how people feel about working the coat check. The ladies' lounge on the fourth floor flooded at some point late yesterday and nobody noticed. There's some water damage on three, but I have maintenance on it. Lastly, the perfume counter somehow managed to run out of Chanel No. 5, which seems like a problem at Christmas."

"A huge problem." Gram would've been horrified.

"Unfortunately, the distributor can't get us anything for a week."

"I'm on it. Can you call a temp agency to see if we can get somebody else to cover the coat check? People stay a lot longer in the store if they don't have to carry around their winter gear."

Lizzie left and Sophie wasted no time getting to work, first taking care of the more urgent matters, like the critical depletion of the Chanel No. 5 supply. After that, she pulled up the previous day's sales numbers, which, although good, weren't where they needed to be. This was one of those instances where she really needed Mindy to help her brainstorm on new marketing and store ideas for next year. But, of course, Mindy hadn't merely expressed her disinterest; she'd said she absolutely refused to help out.

Lizzie rapped on Sophie's door. "It appears that Jake Wheeler has taken things to the next level."

"What now? Giant gourmet fortune cookies?"

Lizzie shook her head. "No. He's here. With flowers. Lots and lots of flowers."

"Here? He's here?" Incomprehensible excitement rushed through her, followed quickly by a dizzying dose of jitters. She hadn't seen Jake in eight years. It had taken three of those to get over him, and even then she wasn't totally sure she'd managed to get him completely out of her system. Knowing what the mere mention of his name did to her made it seem that much more unlikely she'd accomplished the task. "What did you tell him?"

"He knows you're here. Sorry, but Marie stopped by to check on your shoes and he heard me say that you were wearing them right now."

"Lots of flowers?"

"Lots and lots."

Sophie sucked in a deep breath and decided it was best to just get this over with. She couldn't hide from him forever, even though she desperately wanted to. "Okay. I'm coming out." She straightened her clothes, admittedly happy she'd worn a sleek, curve-hugging black dress. Jake didn't need to know that it was one of the more comfortable work outfits she owned. All he needed to know was that she looked amazing in it, and unless he'd lost some visual acuity in the last eight years, he should have no trouble seeing that.

The problem was *she* wasn't prepared to see *him*, especially not as she marched into the reception area and was confronted by his face, somehow more handsome eight years later, poking out above an armful of her favorite flowers—pink peonies. It was as if her subconscious had constructed this scene to disarm her. To leave her as a puddle on the floor. Between the heady smell of the flowers and the mind-blowing sight of Jake, she was surprised she could still stand.

His dark hair was just as thick and unruly as ever. Good God, she'd spent an embarrassing amount of time fantasizing about running her fingers through it. And when she'd finally had the chance, it was even better than she'd imagined. "Hi, Sophie. It's been a long time." His penetrating green eyes broke her down as he unsubtly checked her out from head to toe. His unforgettable mouth pulled into a self-assured grin, one that said he was greatly enjoying the fact that he'd made it into her office. They were finally face-to-face.

"It has been a long time, hasn't it?" Sophie stood a little straighter, but it was just a defense mechanism. She'd forgotten how vulnerable it made her feel to meet his appraisal. Aside from a beautiful pair of black leather wingtips and the hem of charcoal-gray trousers, every other part of Jake was obscured by the flowers. The war that raged inside her whenever Jake popped into her head, or now, her world, was reignited. He knew what he was doing. He knew exactly how weak she was for sweet gestures and sentimentality. This wasn't about expressing his feelings. This was about Jake Wheeler getting what he wanted—his hands on Eden's Department Store.

"I brought flowers."

"So I gather. First fruit, now this?" Sophie planted both hands on her hips, wanting to come off as powerful. Invincible. Certainly as someone who could never be hurt. She dug the heel of her shoe into the office carpet, noting that he couldn't resist the chance to look at her legs. Once again, Mr. Blahnik had done his job.

Jake laughed. "I'm working my way through all the best gifts that start with the letter *f*. Not sure I'm prepared to invest in a Ferrari, though, judging by your reaction to the flowers. I might just go with a ferret."

Sophie was trying to contain her smile. His quick wit had always gotten to her, but it was yet another of his considerable assets, one that he would likely use to soften her defenses. "You're terrible. You think you can just show up at my office with the world's largest arrangement of my favorite flowers and I'll just talk to you?"

"As a matter of fact, I do."

The heat was rising in her cheeks, making her all the more determined to keep this a short visit. She had a million things to do and Jake was nothing but trouble, however nice it was to look at him. "Ten minutes. That's all you get."

"How about ten minutes to catch up and ten to talk business?"

"This isn't a negotiation. We'll spend ten talking business and then you can leave." She wasn't interested in catching up or reliving old times. It was too painful to think about how over-the-moon she'd been for him and how effortlessly he'd rejected her.

"Okay. But what about the flowers? It would be nice to put them down somewhere. Or at least feel like you appreciate them. Peonies are not available in Manhattan in the winter. I had to have them flown in."

His words hit her in one fell swoop. This man she had once cared about deeply had been jumping through considerable hoops to get to her. His motives might be questionable, but perhaps she needed to stop being an ice queen about it. "I'm sorry. I do appreciate them. They're beautiful."

She took two careful steps toward him, not sure whether she should look at him or the peonies. With every inch closer to Jake, she felt herself fall under his spell a little more. She reached for the flowers, but they were so bulky that he had to lean unimaginably close to lay them in her arms. The penetrating gaze of his green eyes left her wondering if this was a dream. Somewhere behind the veneer of expensive gifts and grand gestures, the well-made wool coat and tempting five o'clock shadow, this man who had once been her entire world was still living and breathing.

"Thank you," she muttered. "They really are gorgeous."

Jake didn't step away. He didn't break the connection between them either, his warm hand on her bare elbow, his lips just as kissable as they'd always been, maybe even more so. "They're nothing on you, Soph. I have to say you look amazing. All this time apart has done you well."

Sophie's knees wobbled. His voice caused a deep tremor that resonated through her entire body. "You look great, too. But you were always handsome. You know that." *Handsome* was such an inadequate word for Jake, it was ridiculous. Perhaps it was because he was so much more than good-looking. There was the swagger. The easy confidence. The glint in his eye that made you feel like you were the only woman in his orbit.

"Doesn't mean I don't like hearing it."

Sophie held her breath. If this were a movie, this would be the part where he'd throw caution to the wind, take her into his arms and kiss her, crushing what might be a thousand dollars in flowers between them. She couldn't let herself get carried away with that particular mental image, so she cast her sights down at the arrangement in her arms and gave them a sniff. "I'd better get these in some water."

She hurried over to Lizzie and deposited them on her desk. "If you could put these in some water, that would be great."

"Absolutely." Lizzie looked past Sophie and eyed

Jake. It was easy to see how much she was appreciat-
ing the view. "Would you like me to hold your calls?"

A good interruption would make for an easier escape if she started to feel overmatched by Jake, but
she had to get through this. She had to listen to his
pitch, try not to let the past creep in and send him on
his way. "I think I'll be fine." She waved Jake on to
her office. "Come on. We'll meet in here."

A certain sense of pride hit Sophie when she
stepped inside. Yes, this job was her birthright, but
she worked hard and her office was impressive, especially now. Reginald and his team had really gone
all out. Each of the six windows in her corner office had its own fresh wreath decorated with flocked
pinecones and berries, tied with a wide white velvet
bow. Sparkly white and silver garland framed the
views of the city beautifully. But the tree was the
real showstopper, decorated with silver glass balls,
tiny white-and-red birds wired to the branches and
more twinkle lights than Sophie had ever seen in a
single application. Every time she looked at the holiday iteration of her office, her heart swelled.

"Please. Have a seat," Sophie said, offering one of
the two upholstered chairs opposite her desk.

"It looks like Christmas exploded," Jake said,
sounding a bit stunned.

"It's beautiful, isn't it?" Sophie stepped behind
her desk, surveying the room and ignoring his poor
choice of words. Surely he didn't mean it in such a
crude way.

"Who did this to your office?"

"Reginald. Our creative director. He really out-did himself. I don't know how I'm going to get any work done at all. I just want to stare at it." She folded her hands in her lap, deciding it was no longer time for small talk. "Now, why don't you say what you came to say."

He slowly unbuttoned his coat and draped it over the back of one of the chairs, still admiring the room. Meanwhile, Sophie was trying not to stare at how incredible he looked in his impeccably tailored suit. He cleared his throat, crossed his leg and sat back in his chair, nothing less than pure, casual confidence. "As you know, you and your sister are in a very unique situation. You are not only set to inherit one of the largest commercial buildings in Manhattan, your grandmother had the foresight and the means to pur-chase the land, as well. You don't come across that every day. I'd like to buy the property. I've already told your sister that I'm prepared to pay 4.5 billion for the land and the building."

Sophie worked with a lot of numbers every day, but that one was a doozy. She knew how much the property was worth, and Jake had clearly done his homework. The offer was in line with market value, but just sweet enough to make her have to think twice. She drew a deep breath through her nose to calm herself enough to deliver her answer. "Thank you, but no."

"You can ask any appraiser in the city. It's a very generous offer. I'm willing to move quickly. I have a small group of partners on this deal and we're prepared to do an all-cash sale."

Sophie found a lump in her throat. That was more money than she could likely ever spend, but this wasn't about cash in the bank, at least not for her. This was about carrying out Gram's wishes. Still, it was a good thing Mindy wasn't here right now because she would strangle Sophie for what she was about to say. "Again, no. But thank you."

Jake smiled and nodded as if she'd just agreed to everything he wanted, a tried-and-true negotiation tactic. She wasn't surprised he was resorting to it. "Maybe it's best if I just let you think about it for a few days. Let that big, fat, delicious number tumble around in your head. Because I can guarantee you that any of these other companies and developers are not in a position to pay what I'm willing to pay." His voice held an edge of determination that betrayed the pleased look on his face.

Still, Sophie had to be firm. "I understand what you're saying, but the answer is no. My grandmother worked too hard for me to simply walk away from it."

Jake nodded slowly again. "I know. She was a legend. At one time, she was one of the most successful businesspeople in the city."

"In the country," Sophie interjected. "Quite possibly the world. There were seventy-six stores in twelve countries at the height of Eden's."

"Yes. And now you're back down to this one store. It was the 1980s. It was a different time. Retail isn't what it once was. Frankly, owning a store this big, at this time, is a disaster waiting to happen. You're going to die a very slow, painful death." He was no longer trying to butter her up. Now he was resorting to cold, hard facts, and Sophie didn't like it at all.

"Always the pessimist, aren't you? You know, I think I'll do just fine on my own. And if I don't, I'll just have to die trying." Sophie pushed back from her desk and stood, sucking in a deep breath. This wasn't how she wanted things to end between them, but end they must. She had to put him on notice that she would not waver. She would not sell to him. She would not allow herself to fall under Jake's spell. "Thanks for coming by. And thank you for the flowers."

He cocked his eyebrows and stood. "And the fruit."

"And the fruit. But none of that was necessary, nor is it necessary in the future. I don't need to come into my office to find a flamingo or feather boas."

Jake stood there looking at her, hands in his pants pockets. It felt like he was trying to tear down the invisible barrier she'd tried to build between them, and she didn't like it. "You know, Sophie. I have the distinct impression that this is about far more than your grandmother."

"What? My refusal to do the deal?"

"That and your general distaste for having me share the same air as you."

Sophie froze. All she could hear was the thunder of her own heartbeat in her ears. So this was how he was going to play this. He wasn't going to politely ignore their history as she'd done. He wanted to dredge it up. Sophie could do that. She didn't have to let him off so easy anyway. "The way things ended between us is difficult to ignore if that's what you're suggesting."

"The last time I saw you was on graduation day. I thought things were fine. We hugged. We wished each other well."

That moment was such a permanent part of Sophie's memories it was as if it was tattooed on her brain. It was still a bit raw, even after all this time. She could still feel the deep longing for him, a tug from the center of her chest that told her he was all she ever wanted or needed, but she'd never have him. *With my very beaten-up heart, I told you that I loved you, and you acted as though I hadn't said it.* "That's not quite how I remember it, but I'm glad you can look back on it so fondly. I was still pretty hurt about the way things played out after our one night together."

Jake's forehead crinkled as his eyebrows drew together. "That was for the best. We both know that wasn't going to go anywhere. I wanted to save our friendship, and I thought I had. Now I'm starting to think I've been wrong all this time."

Sophie shook her head. "Of course you felt as though it was up to you to save us from each other. No need for discussion or a conversation. Just a few parting words to get you off the hook, right? It might take two to tango, but only one person has to call it off."

"If it upset you that much, you should've said

something at the time. You seemed completely fine with it."

"I didn't really have time to absorb it. You practically broadsided me."

"Trust me. You're a happier woman right now than you would've been if things had continued."

Anger began to bubble under Sophie's skin. He had no way of knowing things would have ended badly between them. If he'd just given them a chance, they could have been happy. They could have had it all. "Ah, well, apparently your crystal ball works great. Mine is off at the shop. But thanks for watching out for me."

Again, he only looked at her, his mind clearly working hard. "You know, if it wasn't completely inappropriate, I would ask if I could kiss you right now."

Sophie's heart seized up in her chest. A kiss? Was he insane? "I thought you were supposed to be saving me from being hurt."

"I know, but I'm just thinking that the first time I kissed you, you melted right into my arms. That was the moment I knew I could convince you of anything."

She dared to peer up into his dangerous green eyes. They swirled with such intensity it was hard to know whether she'd be able to remain standing or if they'd simply sweep her away. She couldn't believe he would so brazenly use her weakness for him against her. "Get out. Get out of my office right now."

"You won't kick out the guy who brought you a bushel of your favorite flowers."

"I'm serious, Jake. Don't make me call Duane from security. He's six foot six, three hundred and fifty pounds, and has a very short fuse."

"Soph, come on. I'm just kidding. You know me. I'm a kidder."

With a jab of her finger, Sophie directed him to her office door. The exit. "The problem, Jake, is that I do know you. I know exactly what you're capable of, which is the reason I have to ask you to leave."

In a daze, Jake stepped off the elevator on Eden's ground floor. He felt a bit like he'd been run over by a truck. His meeting with Sophie had not gone well, but even more than that, he'd forgotten what being around her did to him. Her sleek black dress was enough to make him sign over his entire business, hugging every gorgeous curve of her body, reminding him of everything he'd had and given up. And that was only the start—her trademark red tresses tumbling over her shoulders, her deep brown eyes blazing and her full cherry-pink lips tempting him into making an admittedly bold remark. It was a business meeting and he shouldn't have brought up kissing. But everything he'd said had been the absolute truth. She had melted into him that night. They were on the same wavelength, completely.

He'd really thought the flowers might do the trick. Sophie was sweet and sentimental. What woman like that doesn't appreciate that sort of gesture? He hadn't expected an immediate yes to his proposition, but he had hoped she would at least consider it. Instead, she'd done nothing more than try to create distance between them. If she'd been any more successful, she'd have had him on the other side of bulletproof glass. It was a real shame. There had been a time when Sophie would come running to him. Not anymore.

He met David, his driver, at the curb and jumped into the back of the black Escalade, his mind a jumble of thoughts of Sophie and business as the sights of the city whizzed by in a blur. He had to turn this around. His killer instinct, the one that had brought him success that surprised even him, wouldn't allow him to back off simply because of one bad conversation. His fellow members of the War Chest were eager to get the jump on this deal, and with each day closer to the reading of Victoria Eden's will, the more unlikely it would be that Jake's plan would work. Everyone in the city with a fat bank account would be pursuing Sophie and her sister by then. If Jake was going to bring this deal to fruition, he had to do it now. Wait and lose out. That was all there was to it.

By the time he reached his office, Jake knew that flowers and fruit baskets had been the wrong approach. He needed to go with reason. She and her sister were sitting on a fortune. All they needed to do was cash in their golden ticket. He needed to show Sophie on paper, in hard numbers, why it was in her best interest to sell. Eden's future was indeed grim. He was certain of it.

"Unless I get a call from Sophie or Mindy Eden, I'm in a meeting," he said to Audrey as he strode past her desk.

"Yes, sir, Mr. Wheeler."

He sat at his desk, pulled out a fresh legal pad, grabbed the folder of background materials Audrey had pulled together on Eden's and opened up a new browser window on his laptop. "Time to figure out just how bad things look for Eden's Department Store."

Hours later, Jake had pages and pages of numbers and notes. He'd read two dozen articles about the future of retail, made estimates as to how much space Eden's was using and wasting with some of their departments. Unfortunately for Jake, the most profitable department, women's shoes, only stirred up thoughts of Sophie in the ones she'd been wearing today. They were some of the sexiest shoes he'd ever seen. For a moment, he had a vision of them on his shoulders and Sophie at his mercy, an idea he immediately wrenched from his mind, although he might be forced to revisit it later.

He moved on to analyzing Eden's online presence and the amount of company resources they were devoting to everything from marketing and advertising to store security and, yes, decorating executive offices like the inside of a snow globe.

This was a bit like reading tea leaves, but he had to make do with what he had, and there was a great deal of satisfaction to take from the knowledge that no other money guy or investor was putting in this kind of work. Sophie would see that he was just looking out for her. He had her best interests at heart.

And himself, of course. This deal would be the talk of developer circles for years. Decades even. And he'd grow his bank account considerably.

But first, he had to call the one person who was on his side—Mindy Eden.

"Jake, I told you the last time we talked, I'm not the one you need to convince. It's all Sophie. I have zero interest in anything having to do with Eden's. I have more than enough on my plate."

Jake tapped his pen on his planner and looked out his office window. The holiday market down in the park was again bustling with people. He'd never understand some people's obsession with Christmas. "Okay. So then tell me how I get through to her. She's not only digging in her heels about the store, she refuses to have a conversation with me."

Mindy laughed. "You do know you broke her heart, right?"

Jake froze as Mindy's words worked their way through his head. "I did not break her heart. Sophie and I had a little too much to drink one night, we had some fun, and I ended it the next day so she didn't have to. Believe me, I was looking out for your sister. Any other guy would've strung her along for months." Did Sophie truly feel as though he'd broken her heart? He'd only tried to protect her.

"Or he might have fallen in love with my perfectly smart and beautiful sister and lived happily ever after."

Not this guy. Jake swallowed hard to stuff those words back inside him. It was one thing to get personal with Sophie, and quite another to talk about subjects like this with Mindy. "Something tells me she would've gotten tired of me real quick."

"Hmm. I don't know about that."

"Do you think it would help to try to talk to her outside of the office? Maybe catch up with her on the weekend when she's more relaxed?"

"You must know that Sophie doesn't relax. I'm not sure a weekend will help you. Plus, she's gone this weekend."

"To where?"

"Our grandmother's house in Upstate, near Scarsdale. It's where the family spends Christmas. She's heading up tomorrow morning."

The wheels in Jake's head were turning. Opportunity was in the air. "Is that the house where you and Sophie spent your summers?"

"That's the one. Eden House."

"Sophie used to talk about it all the time. She seemed to have a lot of great memories from being there."

"We both do, but yes, Sophie loves it. She goes every chance she gets."

"Are you going up this weekend, too?"

"I told her I'd drive up Saturday night. The weather's not looking good, but I think she'll kill me if I don't show up."

This might be perfect—drive up Friday and convince Sophie, Mindy arrives Saturday and they would work out the rest of the deal. The commotion of Eden's wouldn't be a distraction, and hopefully Sophie would be more relaxed and open to the things he had to say to her.

Also, it was clearly time to smooth her ruffled feathers. He hated that she might have been harboring ill will toward him all these years. He'd truly had her best interests in mind when he'd called off their romance before it had a chance to start. He wasn't about to delve into specifics or dig up his own past. There were too many unhappy memories to be found. But he could at least remind Sophie that they had once been very close. He could at least show her that they could, in fact, get along and find a way to help each other.

"So, Mindy. I'm wondering if you can help me with something."

"Sure. What?"

"I'm going to need the address for Eden House."

Three

The instant Sophie turned onto the winding private drive leading to Eden House, she felt more like herself. Her Bentley Bentayga SUV crept silently ahead as the family estate came into view—graying cedar shakes trimmed in crisp white, with three stone chimneys poking up from the gable roof, all of it surrounded by a maze of manicured hedges. Sophie had nothing but the happiest of memories here—endless sunny summer days in the pool, leisurely morning strolls through the rose garden with Gram, rainy days of gin rummy and evenings spent roasting marshmallows over the fire pit on the backyard terrace. Soon this house would be hers, bequeathed to her by her grandmother. Would it ever again be filled with love and laughter? This Christmas was the first big test, and she was terrified that she'd fail.

Sophie and Mindy had spent every Christmas of their lives at Eden House. The family tradition went back to Gram's childhood when her parents had built the house, although it wasn't given the name Eden until Gram inherited it years later as a married woman. Her parents had done well for themselves in the 1950s, importing and wholesaling fabrics for the garment industry. The entire country was booming then, and if you were somebody, you had to have a vacation home. It was simply what you did to show the world that you were a success.

Sophie pulled around to the side entrance and parked her car under the porte cochere in order to ferry the groceries straight into the kitchen. As soon as she opened her car door, she was hit by a bracing cold, the wind whipping past her, picking up the tails of her coat and tossing her hair into disarray. The clean but icy smell of snow was in the air. The forecast was for a fast-moving system that would leave behind one to two inches. Sophie wasn't too worried. In some ways, it would be a dream to get snowed in at Eden House. The power lines were buried, so the electricity rarely went out. She had her cell phone and internet if she needed to get any work done, and there was more than enough wine in the family cellar. A day or two where she was forced to stay away from the store might do her good.

Sophie struggled with the house key, her arms loaded down with shopping bags and her fingers freezing from the cold. She nearly fell through the door and into the kitchen when the lock finally turned. She plopped her bags down on the large center island and opened the Sub-Zero fridge to put away her perishables. That was when the tears started.

The refrigerator was nearly empty, but there on the second shelf were three bottles of Krug champagne. Gram adored champagne, especially Krug. She would've sipped it morning, noon and night if it were in any way socially acceptable. Sophie took one of the bottles from the shelf and smoothed her fingers over the familiar gold foil label. This was an iconic image from her childhood, when champagne was an exotic drink meant only for grown-ups. Gram had brought these bottles up in early October in anticipation of the family's Christmas celebration. And now she wouldn't be there to enjoy them.

Sophie carefully slid the bottle back into place, wiped her tears from her cheeks and put away her groceries. Countless memories of her grandmother would crop up this weekend, and she needed to pace herself. Gram would want her to unwind and not dwell too much on sadness. She'd had an unwavering belief in the power of positive thinking. Life was so much more enjoyable if you could just find a way to be happy. Bad things would happen, but the sun always came up the next day and, somehow, life went on.

Sophie grabbed her suitcase out of the car and lugged it inside. It was snowing now—fat, fluffy flakes. She'd better call Mindy. Her sister was not the type to pay attention to the weather.

"Are you there?" Mindy asked when she answered her phone.

"Just got here, and it's snowing. I checked the forecast and now it's saying at least four inches. Maybe more. I really think you should consider leaving earlier than tomorrow morning. I'm worried the roads won't be passable."

Several moments of background noise filtered through from her sister's side of the line. "There's no way. Things are crazy busy here."

"But you're the boss. You have to take a break sometime, and this is the weekend to decorate the house. There won't be another one." With every new word from Sophie's mouth, she started to feel a bit more panicked. She cared deeply about following through on the family tradition. "I can't do it by myself. I don't want to do it by myself. It's not right."

"First off, I have no doubt that you can do it yourself. Second, there's a chance you won't have to."

"So you'll knock off early and get your butt up here?"

"No. I'm sticking to my plan to leave tomorrow. But there's a chance you might run into Jake."

"Run into him? Where?" Sophie's heart leaped into her throat.

"I don't know. The kitchen? The sitting room?"

"What did you do? Did you send him after me?"

"As serious as you are about not selling, I'm just as determined to change your mind."

A swarm of conflicting emotions buzzed in Sophie's head—anger, frustration and the familiar flutter of anticipation that had become synonymous with seeing Jake. How Sophie wished that part of her brain would stop being so hard on her. "I can't believe you would do this to me."

"I wouldn't if it was a stranger. But you know Jake. You've known him forever. I just think he wanted the chance to talk to you alone."

The word echoed all around her—*alone, alone, alone.* "He won't come. He has too much pride to grovel."

"He showed up at your office with dozens and dozens of peonies, didn't he? Sounds to me like he'll do anything to make a good impression on you."

Sophie shook her head and started down the center hall, with its herringbone brick floor and wide white baseboards. She could already smell the fresh pine of the Christmas tree she'd asked Barry, the Eden House caretaker, to deliver. The fragrance alone lifted her spirits, all while the idea of Jake trying to make an impression aggravated her. He'd never really tried before now, certainly not eight years ago when she'd wanted it more than anything. So what had changed? The promise of a big deal. That was all Jake cared about. Any overtures he made were not only designed to manipulate her and pull at her heartstrings, they were solely prompted by money. She couldn't let him play with her like that. "I have to go."

"Are you mad, Soph?"

"Of course I'm mad. You put me in Jake's cross-hairs. You know how badly he hurt me. He broke my heart."

"I know that. I reminded him of it when we talked."

"You did?" Sophie stepped into what Gram had always called the sitting room. The tree was in the corner, waiting to be trimmed, all while Sophie was overcome with the sort of embarrassment that haunts a teenage girl forever. "He already doesn't take me seriously as a businesswoman. Why did you have to bring our romantic past into it?"

"Because he's a clueless man. He couldn't figure out why you were giving him such a hard time."

"I don't want to sell. This has nothing to do with romance."

Mindy tutted as if she was scolding Sophie. "You really expect me to believe that? Because I don't. Your history with him is clouding your judgment, and you need to get past that. Not just for my sake, but for yours. I think it'll be good for you two to finally talk things through. Clear the air."

Sophie trailed over to one of the tall leaded-glass windows overlooking the sprawling yard. What she could see of the grounds was already covered in a thin blanket of white, with the storm steadily adding more layers. In the spring and summer, this was a lush green vista that had always seemed to go on forever—much like her feelings for Jake, the ones that she desperately wished would just end. "There's nothing for Jake and me to talk about. I already know how he feels about me."

"And how is that, exactly?"

"He sees me as sweet, gullible Sophie. The woman who would do anything for him. I'm not that girl anymore. I won't let him trick me into being her, either."

Mindy grumbled. "Just listen to him if he shows up, okay? That's all I ask."

"As long as you promise you'll still try to come up tomorrow."

"I'll do my best. I'll give you a call in the morning with an update, okay?"

"Fine."

"Love you, Soph."

"Love you, too." Sophie hung up and drew in a deep breath, blowing it out through her nose. She considered calling Jake and telling him to not come, but maybe Mindy was right. Maybe it was time for the two of them to really hash things out. Maybe that would finally let her forget him for good.

In the meantime, Sophie didn't dare start the decorating until Mindy arrived tomorrow. Plus, after her long drive, and her hellish workweek, she was simply exhausted. A nap wasn't merely in order; it was a necessity. She grabbed her suitcase and headed upstairs.

Eden House slept twenty people comfortably, which meant that Sophie and Mindy had always each had their own bedroom. Sophie's was the second on the right in the upstairs hall, directly across from Gram's master suite. It was beautifully decorated in white and soft tones of gray and pink, with a cloud-like four-poster bed and the most picturesque view of the backyard and woods beyond. Sophie changed into comfy lavender silk pajama pants with a tank top and climbed under the fluffy comforter. Not bothering to set the alarm on her phone, she closed her eyes, let her head sink into the feather pillows and tried as hard as she could not to think about whether or not Jake was going to turn up on her doorstep.

When Sophie woke, the room was much darker. From somewhere beyond her door, she'd heard a banging sound. *Bang bang bang.* She bolted up in bed and clutched the covers to her chest, her brain slowly whirring to life. How long had she been asleep? She fumbled for her phone. Her nap had lasted for hours. *Bang bang bang.* Sophie jumped. Then she heard the more pleasant ring of the doorbell and she realized what all that banging was. Jake.

She grabbed a thick cream-colored cardigan, tucked her feet into her boiled-wool slippers and hurried down the hall. As she descended the staircase, clutching the banister, she craned her neck, trying to see through the sidelight. The snow was coming down so fast now it was impossible to make out much more than a dark jacket and a tall figure.

Was it Jake? Logic said yes, but what if it wasn't? Sophie was not a paranoid person, but if that was a strange man out there, she'd better be prepared. She was all alone in this house, practically a sitting duck. Frantically, she scanned the foyer for something to defend herself with. Nothing too scary. She just needed a little insurance. Unfortunately, everything her eyes landed on was too bulky, like a lamp, or useless, like a book. Then she spotted the cast-iron fleur-de-lis doorstop next to the front door. It was heavy but fit into her hand nicely. It would have to do, although she couldn't imagine having the nerve to ever hit anyone with it. The threat was most important, she decided.

Gripping it tightly in one hand, she held it flat against the side of her leg. With her other hand, she flipped the dead bolt and unlocked the door.

Icy cold rushed in with a gust so fierce that she fell back on her heels. Before her stood the most handsome mirage she'd ever seen. Jake. In a puffy black coat and a gray stocking cap that made his eyes look even more intense, like he was seeing right through her. "Jake? What are you doing here?" Of course, she knew the answer. She just wanted to hear it from his mouth.

His shoulders were bunched up around his ears. The wind whipped, sending snow flying past him and into the foyer. "Can I come in?"

Her heart pounded in her chest. "Yes. Of course." She opened the door wider, watching as he stepped inside and stomped the snow from his feet. "What are you doing here?" Again, she waited for the answer. Jake was here because there was no way he was going to give up after their one conversation in her office. He had no problem walking away from Sophie the woman, but he couldn't leave Sophie the business deal alone.

Her hand dropped to her side. The doorstop plummeted, landed square on her foot and tumbled to the floor with a thud. "Ow!" Sophie's foot crackled with unimaginable pain. She jumped and raised her injured foot, hopping her way over to the staircase. Jake mercifully shut out the cold behind him.

"Soph. Are you okay?" He rushed over to her. His voice held enough true concern to make her feel light-headed.

Sophie wasn't sure where to look. At her injured foot or at Jake. "Why did you have to show up and make me drop a doorstop on my foot?"

"Why are you walking around the house with a lead weight in your hand?"

"If you were an intruder, I was planning to knock you out with it."

"I guess I should have called first, huh?"

"That would've been nice."

He dropped to his knee and tugged off his gloves, setting them on the stair tread. He reached for her foot. He was so close now, his cheeks bright pink from the cold, but the rest of his face had its normal tawny tone, the one that looked so perfect with the dark scruff on his jaw. She had an irrational desire to touch it.

"Can you take off your slipper so I can look at it?" Impatient Jake didn't wait for her; he simply removed it himself.

"You still haven't told me what you're— Ow!" She recoiled from the pain.

He held his hands up in surrender. "Sorry. I just… I think we need to get some ice on this and get it elevated. There's a chance you broke your foot." He stood, tugging off his hat and rolling his broad shoulders out of his jacket. To her horror, he tossed them onto her grandmother's upholstered settee.

"Jake. That's velvet and there's snow on your jacket. The water will leave a mark on the fabric." She knew she was being a pain in the butt, but she couldn't help it. He was being thorough, determined Jake—the guy who never gives up on what he wants, no matter what it takes. She had to remind him that he was on her turf. If there was an upper hand to be had here, it was hers.

"We need to get your foot elevated. Can I carry you somewhere so you can lie down?"

The idea of lying down near him had her thinking all sorts of crazy thoughts—she nearly answered that her bedroom was right upstairs. Nearly. She needed to retrain her brain to stop thinking about him that way. There had been a time when she was skilled at keeping herself in the friend zone, but she was out of practice. "I can walk." She had no idea if that was true. Her foot was throbbing like it had its own heartbeat.

"I'm sure you can. But I'm not going to let you hurt yourself when I can stop it."

"So I'll sell you my two billion dollars in Manhattan real estate?" She might as well just put it out there. His true intentions would go far in reminding her that however gorgeous and sexy he was, Jake was a threat to the future she wanted for herself.

"No. So you'll listen to me when I say that I need to

hide out here for a few hours until the storm passes."
Placing his knee on the tread immediately below her,
he reached out for her. "Come on. Put your arm around
my shoulders."

Sophie was prepared to protest some more, but
this close, Jake's heady scent filled her nose, and
that switched her brain into a far too accommodating
creature. She'd long ago developed a serious weakness for his heavenly smell of soap and sandalwood,
and the years apart had *not* managed to dull her reaction to it. Sophie raised her arm and he came in
closer, making the fragrance even more intense. He
wrapped his hand around her waist and scooped up
her legs with his other arm. She had no choice but
to curl her other hand around his neck and turn her
face into his chest as he straightened and picked her
up from the stairs.

"Where to?" he asked.

Sophie was too mesmerized by the sensory de-
lights of being this close to Jake to think of an immediate answer. He was wearing the softest black
cashmere sweater, which was a delicious contrast
to the way his facial hair scratched at her temple.
His body radiated so much warmth, she just wanted
to stay like this. Everything about him seemed designed to draw her in. "Across the hall. The arched
doorway."

Jake carried her into the sitting room. "I'm going
to set you down on the couch." His warmth quickly
evaporated as he let go, a very real reminder of what
a disappointment it was when he decided to step

away. He grabbed a pillow for behind her back and another to go under her foot. "Now ice?"

"Kitchen. Straight down the center hall. You'll find it."

He sauntered out of the room while Sophie took the opportunity to watch him walk away. Talk about a man who looked good coming and going—that was Jake. It was as if his butt was made for those jeans. But now that she was alone, doubt and reality crept back in, reclaiming their stake on her. Jake had a motive for being here, and no amount of admiring him in those jeans or breathing his inebriating scent was going to change it. Jake wanted to buy her dream out from under her, and she wasn't going to let that happen.

Jake found the ice with no problem. It was his confidence that was escaping him.

"What am I doing here?" he mumbled to himself. "This was so dumb. How desperate could I possibly look?" No answers came—spoken or otherwise. He opened several drawers until he located a dish towel to wrap up the compress for Sophie. He found himself almost glad that she'd hurt her foot. It gave him a diversion so he didn't have to answer her questions, but he knew they were coming. She never let him off the hook.

"Here we go," he said, waltzing into the room as if this was a casual meeting of the minds and it wasn't strange that he'd driven hours to get to her. He sat at the far end of the couch and carefully slipped his hand under her foot. Touching her bare skin made a long-gone recognition flicker to life inside him. He looked up at her and their gazes connected, completing a circuit, or at least that was the way it felt on his end. He quickly looked away. He had no business feeling this way about Sophie. Whatever heat and desire that had once been between them might still be smoldering, but he couldn't allow it to burst into full flame. One time, however amazing, was history. Nothing more.

He gently placed the ice pack on what was now a bulging red bump.

She winced. "Do you think I broke it?"

"Can you move your toes?"

She managed a wiggle. "A little. It hurts, though."

"How much does it hurt?"

"I don't know. I've never broken a bone before."

"Seriously? I broke my left arm twice before my tenth birthday." As a kid, he was always getting into trouble while running around the neighborhood, but that was preferable to being in the house. His home life had been lonely and unhappy, especially after his mom left him with his grandmother and never came back. He didn't like to think about it too much, even when he fully owned that it had made him into the man he was today. Independent. Determined. Untrusting.

"I was not rough-and-tumble, Jake. I was the girl reading fashion magazines and thinking too much about boys."

"But then you ended up in business school."

"That was Gram's idea. It was always her plan to groom Mindy and me to run Eden's." Sophie shifted in her seat and looked right at him, chipping away at his resolve with her warm brown eyes. "I know that's why you hunted me down."

So much for small talk. At least he didn't have to sidestep topics or make excuses. "I wouldn't say I hunted you down so much as I used the resources at my disposal to find you."

"I talked to Mindy. I think she was hoping that sending the hot handsome guy to distract me might make me give in to the idea of selling."

A smile played at the corner of his mouth, but he tried his damnedest to suppress it. He shouldn't be happy that she'd called him hot or handsome. "I don't know what her thought process was, but I know she understands that the three of us can help each other. A lot."

Sophie frowned. "So that really is the only reason you're here. One more attempt to get me to give in to you."

The thought of Sophie giving in to him…well, it was too much to take. He'd never get any business done, or repair this friendship, if he was focused on that. "That was part of it. Sure. But I also hate the idea that I can't call your office and get you to pick up the phone. I don't like the fact that I went to see you and it was like our friendship had never existed."

"My grandmother died a month ago, Jake. Believe it or not, this is about more than you and me and our history."

"But we were close once, Soph. Really close."

"*Were*, as in past tense. A lot of years have gone by, during which I heard from you exactly zero times."

"The phone works both ways. I could say the same thing for you."

Sophie jerked her foot back from Jake's hand. "I had my reasons." She leaned on the sofa arm and attempted to stand up. "Ow." She slumped back down on the cushions. "I can't have a broken foot. I don't have time for it. I have too much stuff to do."

"Hey. Easy. It's Friday." He glanced out the window, where the snow was coming down even harder than it had been fifteen minutes ago. "By the look of things, neither of us is getting out of here anytime soon."

"Was it snowing when you left the city?"

"It was. Not too bad."

"And you kept going?"

He'd thought about turning back once or twice, but two things kept him from doing that—first, his promise to his fellow investors that he would close this deal this weekend, and second, he wanted to spend time with Sophie. That line about hating the fact that she wouldn't take his calls was true. He didn't want her to hate him. "The forecast said it was only supposed to be a few inches."

"There's practically a foot out there already."

"I'm sure it'll slow down soon."

Sophie sat back against the sofa cushion. "Do you mind starting a fire? It's a bit drafty in here."

Jake was perennially hot, but if memory served, Sophie got cold all the time. "Sure thing." He hopped up from the sofa. "Where's the wood?"

"Utility room off the kitchen."

He hustled down the hall, found the wood, a stack of newspapers and a carrier. Supplies in hand, he headed back to the sitting room. He stopped for a minute to look at a few of the family pictures in the hall. One in particular held his attention—Christmas morning. Sophie looked to be about thirteen, with spindly legs and a mouth full of braces. Also there were her sister and parents, as well as her grandmother. Each face was so happy Jake found it hard to believe it was real. His own memories of Christmas looked nothing like that. How fortunate Sophie had been to grow up with that in her life—something she didn't have to doubt or question. Jake would have done anything to have had that when he was a kid.

"I can't believe Mindy sold me out," Sophie said as he returned to the room.

He opened the flue and stacked the wood across the cast-iron grate. "I called her after our run-in at your office. I thought an in-person conversation was better than one where you're unbearably busy and a million people are running around." He crumpled newspaper and tucked it between the logs, then used one of the long fireplace matches to start the fire.

"So you wanted to separate me from the herd."

He slid the fireplace screen into place and joined her back on the sofa. "From where I sit, you're already separated from the herd. You're trying to steer a sinking ship all by yourself. And the one person who could help you, your sister, wants nothing to do with it. I don't see how you're going to do it. What happens if she demands a buyout?"

Sophie collected her long hair in her hand, draping it over one shoulder. Jake had always been so mesmerized by the color. He had a serious weakness for blondes and for redheads. Sophie's color was somewhere in between, and he'd never seen that particular shade on anyone, making her doubly alluring. "I guess I'll have to figure out a way to raise the money or propose a payment plan. She is my sister. I'm sure she'll work with me."

"I don't know. She could really use that money for her business. It's important to her."

"My business is important to me, too. Everybody acts like this is no big deal and it feels like life or death to me." Her tone bubbled over with desperation. It was clear that all she wanted was for someone to hear her. She must be awfully tired of Mindy's not listening.

Jake had come to Eden House prepared to show Sophie the problems with the sustainability of her business, but this might not be the time to share everything he'd learned. Plus, one could argue that pointing out the trouble spots would only help her turn things around. He had a loyalty to her, but his first responsibility was to himself and his fellow investors. "I'm sorry. I don't want to upset you."

"Look. Here's the deal. Nothing about Eden's can even be decided until the will is read on December 18. Can we just agree to not talk about the sale until after that day? I don't want to be stuck in a house with you if we have this hanging over our heads."

This was a clever move on Sophie's part, one he hadn't seen coming. He took a moment before responding. He had to cover his own butt. At the very least, his fellow investors expected him to get a leg up on any other potential buyers. "Make me one promise?"

"That depends." She cocked an eyebrow at him. "But I'm listening."

"Promise me you won't make a deal with anyone else without first talking to me. Please don't pull the rug out from under me. I shouldn't even admit this. I know I'm just showing my cards, but chances are that I will always be able to sweeten the deal."

She eyed him with an overwhelming sense of distrust. It felt as though she was peeling back his layers, which made him extremely uncomfortable. "I'll have your back as long as you have mine. Trust is just like the phone. It goes both ways."

Jake sensed this was as close as he'd get to a victory. At least for today. "Does that mean you're willing to mend fences?"

"I'm willing to try. I think champagne might help."

Four

Sophie was proud of herself. She'd found a way to get Jake to back down about Eden's, albeit only a temporary fix. As for their friendship, was it a good idea to repair it? Was it even possible? Her doubts mostly stemmed from the hurt she was still clinging to after eight years. She could admit that much to herself. But it wasn't as simple as forgiving and forgetting. Her attraction to him was still bubbling away inside her, and now that she was back in close proximity to him, there was no telling when she might just boil over and do something stupid like kiss him. Or beg him to take off his sweater. Maybe give her a naked back rub. Stuck together until Mother Nature stopped it with the snow and the road conditions improved, there was no telling what she might do.

"You stay put," he said. "I'll get everything from the kitchen if you just tell me what I'm doing."

"It might be easier if I go with you."

"You want me to carry you again?"

A fun idea, but she needed to maintain her independence. "Maybe you just let me put my arm around your shoulders and I'll hop along on one foot."

The corners of his mouth turned down in the most adorable way. "I'm not sure."

"I'm a grown woman, Jake. I think I can take the risk." Using the arm of the sofa, she pushed herself to standing, balancing on her one good foot. "Should I see if I can put any weight on the bad one?"

He shook his head. "No way. Let's save some excitement for tomorrow." Stooping lower, he wrapped his arm around her waist. His touch was tentative, as if he was recognizing the walls still towering between them. She hated that they were there, but she'd been the one who'd spent so much time and effort shoring them up. And they *did* protect her. There was no discounting that.

She followed his cue, gently draping her arm across his firm shoulders. She leaned into him, and they ambled down the corridor, Sophie traveling one hop at a time. She used a hand to steady herself on the wall, but otherwise depended on him. If this wasn't a metaphor for the first two years of their friendship, she wasn't sure what was. She'd always felt a step behind him, and as if he would always be more capable. One more reason to be glad they'd agreed to table any discussion of Eden's. She despised being at a disadvantage, especially when what was on the line meant so much to her.

"I noticed some of the pictures," he said, gesturing to the wall. "Looks like you had some nice times with your family here."

"The best."

Jake stopped right in front of the one of Mindy and her standing by the pool. This particular snapshot had always made Sophie cringe. She was thirteen and Mindy fifteen. The vast differences in development between girls at those two ages was so evident, it was like a before-and-after picture. Mindy had real hips and breasts, curves and confidence. Sophie was flat-chested and board-straight, incapable of filling out her pink two-piece.

"I love this one," he said.

"You would. This is the only one I hate. Gram thought it was cute."

"It *is* cute. You're adorable with your braces and those long legs."

"What? No. There's nothing adorable about it. I'm so awkward, it's painful to look at."

He shrugged, studying the photograph. "I don't think it's awkward. I can see the beginnings of the beautiful woman you eventually become." He traced his finger along the lines of her body in the photo. "I can see where every curve will eventually be. Knowing what you look like now, the transformation is remarkable."

It wasn't often that Sophie's opinion of anything having to do with herself could be changed or turned around, but he had a point. She'd always looked at the photograph and allowed herself to feel dragged back to the days when she wasn't confident in the way she looked, rather than taking stock in how far she'd come. "I never thought of it that way."

"Most people don't see themselves the way the world does, but I've always suspected you might be one of the worst at it."

"What does that mean?"

"You don't give yourself enough credit for anything. You never have."

"If you're trying to flatter me to get me to soften my view on selling Eden's, it won't work."

He looked down his nose at her, admonishing her with his piercing green eyes. "We agreed not to talk about it, remember? We're supposed to be on a mission for champagne."

"You're right. I'm sorry." He tugged her away from the photograph and they finished their trip to the kitchen. Sophie used the counters to help herself get around the room as she directed Jake to the refrigerator. "There's some amazing cheese in the fridge. Smoked Gouda and Camembert with truffles. Grab that while you're in there and I'll get some crackers."

"Sounds like dinner."

"That was pretty much my plan. It's not fun to cook for one."

Jake nodded. "I know that all too well."

Sophie had to wonder how it was possible that after all this time, they were both still single. She'd had a few near misses over the years, but no one who'd meant enough for her to be devastated that it hadn't worked out. No, she'd used up all her devastation and crushed feelings on the man standing in her kitchen. "The Krug is right on the shelf. It was supposed to be for Christmas, but it'll only be Mindy, myself and our mom this year. I doubt we'll drink three bottles on our own."

"Mindy said you usually come up for the weekend to decorate the house. Why go to that much work if it's such a small celebration?"

"It wasn't always small. When I was little, my grandfather was still alive, and it's only been five years since my dad passed away. Gram had friends who would come and visit, too."

"At Christmas?"

"Sure. You know, people who weren't able to celebrate with their own families, for whatever reason. She never wanted anyone to be alone, but especially not on that day." Sophie hopped over to the pantry and got a box of water crackers then took a small silver serving tray that was tucked back in a cabinet. "What about you? Do you still go home to San Diego?"

Jake brought his findings from the refrigerator. "I've never gone back."

"What? Never?"

"Aside from a business trip a few years ago, I haven't gone back."

Sophie leaned against the counter and stared at him, trying to understand what could possibly keep a person away from home. "But that's where you grew up, right?"

"It is. But I don't have deep ties to it. It's just a city."

"What about your family?"

He cast his sights down at the floor for a moment. "I don't like to talk about it. We should get you back to someplace where you can sit."

Sophie's brain and mouth were now engaged in a tug-of-war—she wanted to ask more questions, badly, but the tone of Jake's answer made it clear this was not a topic he cared to discuss. "Okay. The champagne flutes are in the bar in the sitting room."

Jake carried their impromptu meal on the tray, while Sophie improved her one-foot mode of travel, again using the wall for balance.

"How's the injury?" he asked.

"It's throbbing a lot less, so I guess that's good." Sophie stopped at the bar, which was right inside the entrance to the room, and with both glasses in one hand, she hopped back to the couch. "This is really going to suck if I can't wear cute shoes to work. It's a big part of my look."

Jake sat next to her and peeled the foil from the champagne bottle. Sophie had forgotten what nice hands he had—large, but nimble. "I noticed. Those shoes you were wearing the other day were pretty spectacular." He popped the cork perfectly, leaving only a tiny wisp of fizz escaping the bottle.

"You noticed?" she asked as he filled her glass and handed it to her. Of course, she'd remembered the way he'd looked at her. She remembered every time he admired her so openly, mostly because it hadn't happened very often.

"How could I not? You have amazing legs. The shoes were the very sexy icing on the cake." With his own glass filled, he turned to her. "To Eden's. Come what may, I wish you nothing but success."

She was painfully aware of her own wariness as a smile crossed her lips. She found it hard to believe that he truly wished her business well. It was in his own interest for her to fail. She took a sip of champagne to dull the reality. The pop of golden bubbles tickled her nose, leaving her light-headed, although it might have been more the effect of Jake than the champagne. "You're smooth, Jake. No wonder you're so successful." She reached over and nabbed a cracker from the box, taking a bite.

"I am not smooth. I'm just me. And I didn't feel smooth in your office the other day. I felt like a bungling idiot."

She laughed quietly. "The flowers were a bit over the top. Beautiful, but a bit much."

He shook his head and pinched the bridge of his nose. "A big miscalculation on my part, but I was trying to get your attention." Jake reclined and draped his arm across the back of the sofa, tempting her to relax in a similar fashion, but that would only put her in a position to curl into him. She didn't trust herself.

"You got my attention with the sneak attack of the comment about the kiss. I never saw that one coming. You caught me completely off guard."

She could only imagine what the surprise on her face had looked like at that moment. It had been the very last thing she'd thought he would bring up, made all the more powerful by the sheer magnitude of the memory. That first kiss had been so momentous it was as if her entire world shifted. Since then, it had only become more cinematic in her head, a movie that clicked by frame by frame and filled her with both happy thoughts and bad memories whenever she revisited it. The jubilation when their lips had first met and she finally had her taste of the man she'd wanted for so long? She still couldn't wrap her head around how good that had felt.

"If it makes you feel any better, I never planned on saying that to you, especially not in your office. It was about the most unprofessional thing I've ever done. I guess that just shows you what a disadvantage I was at that day."

Sophie downed the last of her champagne. "You're never at a disadvantage. You knew it would put me off my game."

Jake finished off his first glass as well, then poured them each a refill. "I only said it because I was standing there trying to figure out how to remind you that there had once been a time when we got along great. And I looked at you and the instant I saw your lips, I thought about the kiss. You can't deny that was a kiss for the ages."

"I don't deny it. At all." The flood of warmth in her body that came from thinking about the kiss only made her angry. *And you threw it all away.*

"I still think about it sometimes."

Sophie narrowed her sights on him. Was that an actual blush of pink on his cheeks? "You do?"

"Well, sure." He took another drink and leaned forward, placing the glass on the coffee table. When he sat back, his hand brushed hers, which was planted on the sofa between them. He pulled his away, leaving her nothing but painfully aware of his effect on her. An instant of touching and he'd stoked the fire inside her, the one that had always burned brightest for him. "Don't you?"

Of course she did. How could he be so clueless about what it had meant to her? She still thought about that kiss and everything that had come after it. She'd thought about it more in the last few days than was probably healthy. "I know what you're doing. You're reminding me of the good and glossing over the bad."

"I'd like to think I'm taking advantage of a chance neither of us ever knew we would have. We're in this beautiful house together. The snow is coming down. There's a fire crackling away. We're drinking champagne and enjoying each other's company."

Was that all this was? What did he want from her? The truth of it, not just what he'd said to make himself look good. Her head was filled to the brim with contradictory answers to both questions. She wanted Jake just as much as she'd wanted him all those years ago. She wanted him as much now as the night he finally gave in. That night was sheer heaven—dozens of tightly held fantasies brought to life. She would have given anything to revisit that feeling, when the world and future felt wide open.

"I should go to bed." She steeled herself and got up from the couch. She had to save herself before she did something dumb and embarrassed herself. It would be too easy to give in to his touch and give away what little power she had.

"You sure? It's early."

"I'm sure."

"Let me help you up the stairs." Jake stood and offered his arm.

She should have refused it, but the truth was that she wasn't entirely steady. Mentally or physically. "Okay. But I need to get back on my own two feet tomorrow."

"There's no reason to push it. You have time."

As promised, he helped her up the stairs. Not a word was uttered. Jake was performing his duty and Sophie was too busy dying on the inside. Why did she have this weakness for him? And if she was meant to suffer with that for all eternity, why did he have to come waltzing back into her life? It didn't seem fair. Why couldn't she find a regular man, one to whom she was attracted a normal amount, one she could count on to stick around?

"Thank you," she said when they arrived at her bedroom door. "I can take it from here."

"I can help you to the bed."

Sophie closed her eyes and wished for strength. "I'm fine hopping my way around."

She let go of his arm, but his hand immediately went to her shoulder. "Sophie, wait."

Her eyes clamped shut again. "What?"

"Downstairs. I thought we were having a good time."

"We were." She swallowed hard and looked at him, wondering if she had the guts to be truly honest and say what needed to be said. "But then your hand touched mine and I started to lose my mind."

"I wasn't trying to make a move, if that's what you're suggesting."

"Then why even bring up the kiss? Why mention it in my office the other day?"

"Because I have incredibly fond memories of that moment. I guess I don't see the harm in being open about the way I feel about it."

Sophie's knees wobbled. If she needed any evidence that she acted erratically when it came to Jake, that reaction was absolute proof. "I don't want you to hide your feelings. But it would be nice if you could acknowledge that when you're traipsing down memory lane, you're digging up an awful lot of painful things for me."

Jake nodded slowly, taking it all in. "I never want to make you feel bad. That's not my intention." His hand was still on her shoulder and his thumb brushed back and forth. "Maybe now is the time to talk about it. Were there things you wished you'd said to me then that you want to say now?"

Sophie unleashed a breathy laugh, if only to relieve some of the pressure built up inside her. How do you tell someone in a single breath that you're mad at them, but you still want them? How do you tell a man that if he wanted you, you were exactly dumb enough to forgive him? "I lied when I said it was fine that you wanted to go back to being friends. I wanted more then. A lot more."

"Oh." His forehead crinkled with concern and more than a bit of genuine confusion.

"Honestly, I thought you were being stupid. But I also wasn't about to argue with you. I didn't want to have to stand there and make a case for your liking me. That's not how it works."

"I've always liked you. I still like you. But it feels like you hate me." He inched closer, almost imperceptibly, but Sophie would have noticed if a single hair on his head had shifted. She was that hyperaware of everything he did.

"I don't hate you. I want to, but I can't."

Now it was his turn to laugh. "That bad, huh?"

She stared up at the ceiling. "Yes. I'm pathetic. I look at you and all these old feelings rush back like they never went away. I'm in the same room as you and I want you just as badly as I did before. Maybe more."

Jake slowly slid his hand from her shoulder down the back of her arm, stopping at her wrist. He rubbed the tender underside with the pads of his fingers. Back and forth in a lazy yet steady rhythm that made Sophie dizzy. The man's hands were magic. "So we're in the same boat. I wanted you the instant I saw you in your office the other day."

"You did?" Red-hot heat flooded Sophie's cheeks. Her breath caught in her chest.

Jake looked right at her with those intense green eyes of his. She felt a little like he was looking right through her. He cupped the side of her face with his hand. It took every ounce of strength not to smash her body against his.

"It's not just because you're beautiful, either. It's more than the big brown eyes and perfect skin and beautiful hair. It's more than your unbelievable body. It's the spark that's inside you. It's the crazy things that come out of your mouth." He swiped his thumb across her lower lip, sending want through her. He inched closer until they were standing toe to toe, now cupping the back of her neck, his fingers curling into her nape. "I loved being able to carry you. I loved having my hand brush yours and seeing the reaction on your face. It all made me want more."

Sophie stared at his full lips. Did she have the nerve to say what she wanted to? If she said something daring and it led them to bed, could she live with it if he rejected her again? Surely that was the path before them right now. She might get a night with Jake Wheeler, but she'd never get a lifetime. "Why should I believe you?"

He reached down for her hand and then did something Sophie never expected. He took it and threaded it under his sweater, holding her palm flat against the center of his chest. "Do you feel my heartbeat?" he asked.

Indeed, she did. She also felt the warmth of his

skin and the firm muscles of his chest. She didn't have words, so she nodded, never taking her eyes off him.

"Good. Now feel how it changes." He raked his fingers through her hair and pulled her closer, planting his lips on hers. He took his time with the kiss, soft and sensuous, silently begging her tongue to tangle with his. All the while, he kept her hand pressed hard against his chest.

Sophie closed her eyes, leaning into him, wanting to keep her hand pinned between their bodies. She curled her fingers into his chest, but she never let her palm move. She felt what he wanted her to. His heart was thumping wildly. She was doing this to him. He really did want more.

"See what I mean?" He kissed her cheek softly, then her jaw and finally her neck.

"I do," she whispered, tilting her head to one side to grant him full access, thinking she might reach her peak from this alone. His mouth on her body felt so impossibly good.

He gathered her hair in his hands and pulled it to one side, leaning into her ear. "Told you I wanted more."

"That's what I want, too." It felt so good to say it.

Jake swept Sophie up into his arms and made the quick journey to her bed, laying her down on the butter-soft bedding, still rumpled from her nap. She scooted back and curled a finger, wanting him closer, wanting his body weight on top of hers.

He reached for the hem of his sweater and pulled

it up over his head. Sophie sucked in a sharp breath. She loved Jake's chest, and after eight years she was not disappointed. He'd clearly spent much of that time at the gym. He was muscled and taut, with contours that just begged to be explored. He sat on the edge of the mattress and stretched out next to her, lying on his side, kissing her like this was everything he wanted. His hand slipped under her cardigan, pushing it from her shoulders. He rolled to his back, pulling her along with him. She straddled his hips and wrestled her sweater from her arms, tossing it to the floor.

"I love that you're already dressed for bed, but I want to watch you take off your top." Jake's voice shook Sophie to her core.

She crossed her arms and peeled the garment up the length of her torso. She hadn't been wearing a bra that whole time, and her nipples, already hard from the simplest of Jake's touches, became impossibly hard when the cool air of the room hit her skin.

Jake groaned his approval and had his hands all over her, cupping both breasts and squeezing. With a tug, he urged her to lower herself until he had one nipple in his mouth. His lips were soft on the firm bud, but his tongue was insistent, swirling in circles that made Sophie feel as though she was already about to burst. She rotated her hips back and forth, rubbing against the firm ridge in his pants. Another gravelly affirmation came from his throat, and Sophie closed her eyes as he moved his mouth to her other breast, repeating those same mind-blowing moves.

As amazing as this all was, she wanted him naked, and if she were being honest, these pajama pants she was wearing were getting in the way, as well. She slid back on his legs, unbuttoned and unzipped his jeans while he tucked his hands back behind his head.

"Feel like you need a rest?" she asked, only half joking.

"No. I just like watching you."

She smiled and tilted her head to the side, her hair falling across her shoulder. She peeled back his jeans and his black boxer briefs, until they were just past his hips. As soon as she wrapped her hand around him, she knew exactly how hard he was for her. She would have been lying if she'd said it didn't make her immensely happy to know that she could still have this effect on him.

His eyes were closed, his head fitful on the pillow and his back arching as she took long, firm strokes with her hand. "That feels so good," he muttered.

Another smile crossed her lips. She loved pleasing him. "Yeah?" She lowered her head and pressed soft kisses against the flat plane of his stomach, keeping her grip and caressing.

"I want you, Sophie. I want you now. But I don't have a condom with me. I didn't exactly plan for this."

She loved the subtle begging tone of his voice. "I have a few in my bathroom." She hopped down and traipsed into the bathroom, opening a drawer and getting what she came for.

"I'm not sure if I should be happy that you're so prepared," Jake called from the bedroom. He was sitting up on the edge of her bed when she returned. His jeans and boxers had thankfully landed on the floor.

"I hate to break this to you, but there were other men in my life after you."

He gave in to his adorable frown. "I'll pretend that you didn't say that. Now come here."

Sophie stepped between his legs, still wearing her silky pajama pants, but nothing else. Jake gripped her hip with one hand while untying the tie at her waist. He poked a finger beneath the waistband and loosened it until her pj's slumped to the floor.

Standing before him, totally naked, she was struck by how surreal this all felt. She'd never thought she'd ever have Jake again. Not once had she dared to truly believe it could happen. And yet here he was. Looking so handsome she could hardly comprehend it.

He lowered a hand to her knee and dragged his palm up the length of her thigh, turning inward as he went. When his fingers found her center, Sophie dragged in a deep breath and held it, waiting to see what he would do. His other hand pulled her closer until her knees were pressed against the mattress, while his fingers moved in determined circles and his mouth, wet and hot, traveled all over her stomach.

Sophie closed her eyes and let her head drop back, giving in to the sensation, letting Jake take her wherever he wanted to take her. She combed the fingers of one hand into his thick and silky hair, rubbing his scalp, wanting him to feel even a small measure of the pleasure he was giving her. The pressure was building in the most delicious way, but she couldn't deny that she wanted all of Jake, not merely his hands or his mouth on her body. She wanted them joined.

She tore open the foil packet in her hands and kissed the top of his head. "I want you, Jake. I want you inside me."

He smiled and leaned back, resting his elbows on the bed and watching as she rolled on the condom. She planted her hands on either side of his hips and kissed him. They both took that kiss as deep as it would go, mouths hungry for each other, tongues winding and playing. Jake scooted back on the bed. Sophie took the invitation and climbed onto the mattress, straddling him. Jake guided himself inside her. Sophie's eyes clamped shut as she felt him fill her completely.

Jake hummed his appreciation. "You feel perfect."

"You do, too." *So perfect. So unbelievably perfect.*

They were both already a little breathless, nothing more than soft moans and gasps. She lowered her torso and kissed him while rocking her hips forward and back. His thrusts were strong but careful, every pass hitting the right spot. Again, she was speeding toward release. His kisses, hot and reckless, only made the pressure coil faster.

Jake clamped his hands onto her hips, curling his fingers into her bottom like he couldn't get enough.

It intensified the pressure, and that brought her right to the brink, her breaths now choppy and desperate.

"Are you close, Soph?" he asked, burrowing his face in her neck and kissing that sensitive spot beneath her ear.

"So close." She could practically see it in her mind, a swirl of intense colors she wanted to become a part of.

Jake took a thrust and flipped her to her back, straightening his arms and using his considerable strength to drive all the way inside her, then nearly all the way out. Sophie arched her back and gave in to the pleasure as it rocketed through her. She wrapped her legs around Jake's waist and muscled him closer with her feet, studying his incredible face while he, too, reached his peak. A smile stretched across his lips as the subtle tremors shook his body. He collapsed on top of her and rolled to his side, pulling her against his chest. He smoothed back her hair with his hand, gently and lazily.

Sophie relished the afterglow and tried so hard to stay in the moment. Was this really happening? Was she really in his arms? It was real, with no reason for her to feel anything but happy and satisfied. There was no reason to let doubt creep back in. There was no reason to wonder if he'd started things simply because he wanted to keep her under his control.

Five

Jake woke up the next morning wondering if he'd messed up. Sophie was not in her bed with him, and the disappointment registered square in the center of his chest, an emptiness that was deeply uncomfortable. That alone scared him. Had he made a mistake by taking her to bed last night? He didn't have the best track record. It was difficult for him to trust, especially a woman.

He'd allowed himself the pleasure of Sophie only after she'd promised not to cut a deal on Eden's with anyone else without first speaking to him. In that moment, he realized that she did still value their friendship. She was still loyal Sophie. And that made him want to trust her.

He rolled to his side and checked her side of the

bed for warmth. Whatever had been there was gone, but her sweet smell wafted into the air when he rubbed his hand across the sheets. They'd had the most incredible night, making love for hours. They'd even managed to use up Sophie's condom supply. It had to have been nearly four in the morning before they drifted off in each other's arms, which made her absence this morning that much more confusing. How could she be up and about on so little sleep?

He decided to investigate, climbing out of bed and putting on his jeans and the T-shirt he'd been wearing under his sweater. Through Sophie's window, he saw the back of the property covered in virgin snow. The sun was out, and apparently the storm had passed. Surely the process of clearing the roads was already under way.

He was starting down the hall when he heard a terrible racket coming from what sounded like the kitchen. He followed the noise through the house, shuffling into the room. "Are you sure you should be walking around on that foot of yours?"

"It's fine. Swelling has gone down." Sophie glanced at him over her shoulder and smiled. Wearing form-fitting black yoga pants with a pale blue sweater that dipped temptingly off her shoulder, she had a vast array of cooking supplies out on the counter.

"What are you doing?" he asked.

"Getting ready to bake Christmas cookies."

"Cookies? It's just the two of us."

"Not back at home it isn't. I'll bring a bunch back

to the city. Take them into the office. I'll freeze some for Christmas Day, too. Want to help?"

Jake saw that the coffeemaker was on. He was going to need caffeine before grappling with the idea of holiday baking. He'd been hoping he'd talk Sophie into coming back to bed. "May I?" he asked, gesturing to the carafe.

"Oh, yes. Of course. I'm sorry. I should have offered. I'm just scattered this morning." She handed him a carton of half-and-half from the refrigerator, watching him as he filled his mug and stirred it. "By the way, I spoke to Barry, our caretaker, and he said the driveway will be clear by night. He checked with the state highway patrol and they're expecting the roads to be fully passable by morning."

There was his answer about how long he and Sophie had together. Once they were headed back to the city, he'd have the unenviable task of telling Sophie that although this was fun, it probably wasn't a good idea considering their opposing viewpoints on a multibillion-dollar deal. "Thank you for the coffee."

"Good?"

"The best."

She smiled and cocked her head to one side. "Last night was the best."

He couldn't believe how relieved he felt to hear that from her. He really had been thrown off his game by her absence this morning. He set his mug down on the counter and pulled her closer, kissing only the tip of her nose since there was no telling how bad his morning breath was. With his hand, he swept tendrils of her hair from her face. "It was amazing. I was hoping for more. There must still be a few dozen positions we haven't tried."

A beautiful pink blush rose in her cheeks. "You sure? I'm pretty sure we went for a world record last night. Plus, we're out of birth control."

"There are other things we can do to make each other happy." He bounced his eyebrows at her.

She nodded. "I know. And that sounds awesome, but I have to get through my to-do list today. Cookies. Decorating."

He had to admire her dedication to upholding family traditions, even if it was getting in the way of what he considered to be a markedly better time. Plus, the entire idea of baking and cookies and decorating for a holiday was a foreign concept. The only long-held practice in his family involved cruel words muttered under one's breath. "Whatever you want to do, I'm good with."

"Really? You'll help? I would've pegged you as the guy who would much rather sit on his butt and watch football all day."

"Football is on Sunday. And I'd still prefer that, but we should probably honor your grandmother's traditions. I never met her, but I'd like to think she'd want us to."

A melancholy smile crossed Sophie's face. "She absolutely would want us to. She'd be horrified if she knew that I ended up going home without a tin of cookies in the back of my car." She drew in a breath that made her shoulders rise. "The butter is probably soft by now, so we can get started."

"Put me to work."

Sophie began the Christmas cookie operation by directing Jake to follow her into a large pantry at the far side of the kitchen. She handed him a stack of metal sheet pans, then piled flour, sugar, baking soda and baking powder on them. "One more second. I need to find the cookie cutters and the sprinkles." Sophie pulled out a small stepladder.

"Why don't you let me do that?" he asked.

"I'll be fine."

"So says the woman who dropped a ten-pound door-stop on her foot." Jake ducked back into the kitchen, put the supplies on the counter and returned to the pantry. Sophie hadn't listened. She was up on the ladder, reaching for items on the top shelf. "I really don't want you to hurt yourself again. I'll feel responsible this time."

"Just come here and let me hold on to you."

Jake stepped closer and Sophie placed her hand on his shoulder. He was facing her side, and if he looked up, he could see the lovely curve of her breasts as her top stretched tighter across her chest. It brought back some very hot memories of last night, and that only made his jeans start to feel much snugger below the waist. Looking straight ahead was no help—he either had to look at the rounded perfection of her backside in yoga pants or the sweet scoop of her lower back as her top shifted up and revealed her creamy skin.

"Here are the cookie cutters." Sophie handed him a large plastic jar filled with silver metal shapes.

Jake took it from her and set it on a lower shelf, returning his sights to her.

"And here are the sprinkles."

"Gotta have sprinkles."

"Lots and lots of them. There is no such thing as too much sugar in this scenario."

All Jake could think was that Sophie was the real sugar in the room. She was so sweet and mouthwatering, it would be a struggle to stay focused on the task at hand, especially when he didn't care about silly things like cookies.

They returned to the kitchen and Jake helped Sophie get out a large stand mixer. He studied her as she worked. She was still limping but otherwise getting around just fine. Her face was both happy and content, but there was something even more mesmerizing about her, something he'd just realized. She was comfortable in her own skin. That was the biggest change between now and when they'd first met. Back then, she'd had this coltish quality—all unbridled beauty. But she hadn't seemed to know that she was, in fact, beautiful. She was a wallflower of sorts, shying away from compliments and always deflecting.

Now was different. She owned her movements, much more comfortable with herself. When they'd made love last night, Sophie was confident in a way she hadn't been before. She wasn't shy about taking pleasure for herself, which he loved. Having her in his arms, her sweet taste on his lips—it was like revisiting the most perfect memory, only better. He and Sophie hadn't been perfect together all those years ago, but he had to wonder if it was all his fault that it hadn't lasted. He'd thought he'd been protecting her. He'd always thought it was so much better to have a little bit of something beautiful than ever risk it getting ugly.

"Have you talked to Mindy?" he asked as Sophie cracked eggs into the mixing bowl.

"She sent me a text this morning. She's not coming, but I get it. The roads are terrible."

Jake nodded. If he and Sophie hadn't come to their agreement, the news of Mindy might be disconcerting, since he'd counted on an audience with her to seal the deal. Now he was glad that she wasn't coming. It meant he had Sophie all to himself. At least for a little while longer.

She stared down into the mixer, then flicked the switch off. "I think that's good. We need to wrap up this dough and let it chill for an hour before we bake."

"We have to wait for cookies?"

She grinned so wide her cheeks were like little apples. "Afraid so. But you can help me with all of the house decorating until then."

"I was hoping to get cleaned up. Maybe take a shower? Together?" He tugged on Sophie's sweater until she was in his arms again.

She returned the embrace and settled her head against his chest. "That sounds amazing. But no." She straightened and patted his shoulder before returning her attention to the cookie dough, wrapping it up in plastic.

"No?"

"As tempting as you are, not right now. Later. I promise."

Grossly disappointed, Jake helped Sophie clean up the kitchen, and then they moved into the sitting room, where cardboard boxes and plastic crates were stacked against one long wall.

"When you come up here for a weekend by yourself, what do you do the whole time? Read? Watch TV? I think I'd go stir-crazy."

"This is actually the first time I've come by myself. Normally, either Gram and I would come or we might drag Mindy along or my mom, although she and Gram never got along."

"How is your mom?" Jake had met her at business school graduation.

Sophie shook her head. "Not well. Erratic. Losing it. Honestly, she just hasn't been herself since our dad died five years ago."

"I was sorry to hear about that."

"Thanks. It was so hard on Gram. No one wants to see their own child die before them."

"Of course not." Again, Jake was struck by how tight-knit her family was. He knew, of course, that many families were. He simply hadn't had such a bird's-eye view of it.

Sophie began opening the boxes and inspecting the contents. "We've always spent Christmas in this house. It's all Mindy and I have ever known. Gram always came up from the city one weekend in December to decorate the house, so it would be all decked out for celebrating. When Mindy and I got old enough to help, we came up with her."

"An entire weekend devoted to decorating for Christmas. Who does that?"

Sophie shrugged, fishing smaller boxes out of the large ones. Judging by the quantity of decorations, they were going to be busy with this for a while. "The queen of England travels to Sandringham Estate a week before Christmas just to prepare for everything."

"The queen of England and about fifty members of her staff. I realize you come from a lot of money, but unless I managed to miss something, you aren't royalty."

"Of course not. But it's still a nice idea, isn't it? The tradition. The devotion to getting the details right. And most important, wanting that family time to be special."

"I guess. But you're just going to have to take it down later. It seems like a lot of work for nothing."

Sophie turned to him with brows furrowed in confusion. "How do you accomplish anything with that attitude? You're a developer, Jake. You build things. You turn a piece of property into something better or different. How can you have that kind of vision and still be so pessimistic?"

He shrugged. "One person's pessimism is another person's practicality."

Judging by the look on her face, she remained unconvinced. "Let's get started. The sooner we finish, the sooner we get to take that shower."

As distracted as Jake was by the promise of soaping up Sophie's beautiful body, he still felt as though he had to come clean about his disinterest in this exercise. "There's something I need to tell you before we start. A confession of sorts."

"What's that?"

"I know you're going to think I'm crazy, but I hate Christmas."

Sophie could hardly compute what Jake had said. Honestly, it was crushing. How could she be so hopelessly attracted to someone who hated her favorite time of year? "You don't hate it. I don't believe that for a minute. Maybe you think it's too commercial or overhyped or something, but I don't believe that you *hate* it. That's such a strong word."

Jake held up his hands and shrugged. He was somehow extra handsome when he appeared defenseless, even when she knew it wasn't real. "Fine. Then don't believe me. But it's the truth."

"So you aren't enjoying this?"

He cocked an eyebrow at her. "I'm just here for the shower."

Sophie was excited by the prospect, but she couldn't fail at this family tradition. Plus, she was still sorting out how she felt after last night. It had been absolutely incredible, and Jake wasn't showing signs of retreat, which had been her greatest fear, but what would happen tomorrow when they left their snowy hideaway? She needed to prepare herself for the worst. He could easily tell her he wasn't interested and she'd have no choice but to accept his decision. After all, she'd known very well what the possibilities were. She'd known all along that Jake might hurt her.

But she couldn't allow herself to think about that now. It would ruin one of her favorite days of the year. She reached for one of the bins. "We need to put the lights on first. Before anything else."

"If you say so."

Sophie wrinkled her nose. It was as if Jake had never done this before. Perhaps he was merely letting his attitude and actions demonstrate his dislike for the holiday. She pulled out several strands of lights, which had all been carefully wound around pieces of sturdy cardboard. She handed Jake the plug end of one. "Let's test these before we put them on the tree."

"Good thinking." He crouched down near the outlet. One by one, he checked to make sure they all still worked.

"Gram was always adamant that only white lights went on the tree. What about your family?"

Jake didn't make eye contact. "I don't really remember."

Sophie decided to accept that Jake simply hadn't taken note of his family's Christmas preparations. Even with her admittedly persnickety placement, they had the tree strung with lights in no time. "You know, plenty of people say that stringing Christmas tree lights is the ultimate test of a relationship." As soon as the words crossed her lips, she knew she'd made a mistake. She and Jake had the strangest, most tenuous of relationships right now—a long-gone friendship only recently rekindled, an apparent weakness for the other, especially when naked, and a business deal Sophie didn't want waiting off in the wings.

"I'd say we did pretty well," Jake said. "But then again, we've always made a good team. We've always worked well together."

Was this one of his sales pitches? Or was it as innocent as it sounded? An admission that they did indeed work well together?

Jake reached for one of the boxes tucked inside the larger carton labeled Ornaments. "Maybe I should hand you these one by one and you can be in charge of placing them on the tree."

Sophie nodded. "Good plan. Less walking for me. But I'll need you to put up the high ones."

An hour later, the tree was trimmed. Jake built a fire while Sophie put out Gram's collection of musical snow globes on the antique console table in the hall. She then sent him into the kitchen to make hot chocolate while she carefully decorated the banister and the mantel, just as Gram had always done, with garland and ribbon. She was admiring her handiwork when Jake returned to the sitting room with the silver tray they'd used for champagne last night, this time topped with mugs of cocoa.

They sat on the sofa, and Sophie was overcome with a deep sense of accomplishment until she realized what was missing. "Oh, my God. Gram's gold star. We forgot to put it on top of the tree." Sophie sat up and hobbled over to the storage containers, rummaging through them, but there wasn't much left. Just some ribbons for the fresh wreaths, which the caretaker would put up next week after she was gone.

"I went through all of the boxes, Soph. I don't remember seeing a star."

"It has to be here somewhere. It has to." Her stomach sank as she reached for the last box and discovered that it, too, was empty. "I wonder if Barry forgot some of the boxes." She turned to look around the room. The only problem with that theory was that the other decor was all up. She didn't want to get unduly upset about a star, but this one was special. "I'm sure this sounds silly to you. What with you thinking Christmas is terrible to begin with."

Jake got up from the couch and went to her, pulling her into a reassuring embrace. She loved being in his arms, even when she knew that getting used to it was a dangerous proposition. "If it's important to you, it's important to me. I'm sorry you can't find it. Hopefully the caretaker can track it down and it can be the first thing you put up when you're here for Christmas."

Sophie gazed up at him. It was still three weeks until the big day, and two until Gram's will would be read. Where would she and Jake be by then? Anywhere? She would've considered inviting him to spend Christmas with her family, if her gut wasn't telling her to set aside expectations and take every bit of enjoyment she could out of her time with him. "You're right. It's got to be here somewhere. I'll let Barry worry about it."

Jake pressed a soft kiss to her forehead, leaving behind a lasting tingle. "That's the spirit."

She smiled. "As handsome as you are, you sort of look like hell, you know. Your hair is a disaster and we should probably try to find you some other clothes to wear."

Jake's eyes darted from side to side. "Was I not the person leading the charge on a shower earlier?"

Oh, yes. That. She took his hand and, even with her slight limp, started to lead him out of the room. "And I'm following through with my commitment."

Without warning, he scooped her into his arms and pulled her tight against his chest. "Hold on, hummingbird." Like a man on a mission, he bounded up the stairs, determined. A few steps down the hall and he delivered her to the bathroom en suite, placing her on the cool white marble counter.

She watched as he opened the glass door and reached in to crank the handle for the water. The sight was exactly like a daydream she once would have readily whipped up in her head—enticing Jake, with two days of dark scruff on his face and a flicker in his eyes, happy and so clearly enthusiastic to be with her, taking off his T-shirt and letting her admire him in just his jeans. Was she, in fact, dreaming? "You haven't called me hummingbird in forever."

A clever smile spread across his face. "You know, you are the only person I've ever given a nickname. Ever." He stepped in between her knees, snaking his arms around her and leaning against the counter.

"Really?" Sophie remembered the day like it was

yesterday, but she hadn't thought about it in forever. It was a glorious late-spring day, warm and sunny, and they'd met at a café to study. On the side of the building was a patio with hanging baskets overflowing with pink and purple petunias. Nearly a dozen hummingbirds buzzed and flitted among the blossoms, drinking the nectar. Jake had said that they reminded him of her. "Busy and fun to watch" were his exact words.

"Yes, really. I am not a nickname sort of guy. But it suits you. It still does." With his thumb, he inched her top off her shoulder and kissed it with his mouth open. The bathroom was beginning to fill with steam. "Now let's get you out of these clothes."

Why Sophie was so touched by this revelation she wasn't sure, other than knowing that she occupied any exclusive space in Jake's life felt very special. She eased off the counter to get undressed. Jake quickly had his remaining clothes in a puddle on the floor. She drew in a deep breath as she looked him up and down. The man was a stunning specimen—long, lean and defined from head to toe—shoulders, chest and abs were only the start. He had an impressive erection, too. She couldn't wait to please him again.

She pulled her top over her head and unhooked her bra while Jake studied her in turn. "Sorry. I'm still a little behind," she said.

He shook his head. "Don't be sorry. I'm enjoying every second of anticipation." Steam billowed out of the shower enclosure, making Jake look that much more like a god.

She shimmied her yoga pants and panties past her hips, taking her time and following his eyes as they traveled down the length of her body. Every subtle approving glance made her feel more special. And lucky. Jake tugged her into his arms and placed a firm kiss on her lips, then took her hand and led her behind the glass door.

The bathrooms had been remodeled six or seven years ago and Sophie's shower was magnificent—with gray and white hand-painted tile in a Moroccan pattern, a white honed marble floor, six multidirectional sprays and more than enough room for two people. Arguably the best feature was a bench at one end, which Sophie used for shaving her legs.

"Sit," Jake instructed. "I'm not taking any chances with you and that foot and slippery surfaces."

"Yes, sir." Sophie did as instructed, while Jake turned in the spray, slicking back his hair and providing her with an unparalleled view as water trickled down his body, following each muscled contour.

Sophie picked up a bottle of body wash and offered it to him. "Here. This will help."

Popping the cap, he gave it a sniff. "Mmm. Nice."

"Coconut. Not too girlie."

"It's perfect. But not yet. I don't want to get any soap in my mouth."

Sophie suddenly found it hard to speak or swallow. The anticipation of what might come next was too much. Jake descended on her, his mouth on hers as he knelt on the shower floor between her legs. He slipped both hands behind her knees and dragged her forward until her bottom was at the front edge of the bench. He kissed his way down her neck and to her breasts, taking her nipple into his mouth and swirling his tongue against the tight skin. Wet heat swirled all around her, while inside her, a fire that could be put out only by Jake had burst into full flame.

He took her breasts into his hands, squeezing and kneading and plucking at her nipples with his fingers while he kissed his way down her stomach. When he passed her belly button, he tugged her even closer to the edge, parted her tender folds with his fingers and nearly sent her off into space with a single pass of his tongue. Sophie's eyes fluttered shut and she dug one hand into his hair while her other hand was flat on the bench for support. Jake worked her apex with his tongue, winding in dizzying circles. He grasped the ankle of her good leg and raised her foot until it was on the bench. She leaned back, resting on her elbow, while Jake placed one hand on her inner thigh and with the other slipped two fingers inside her.

Sophie could hardly keep up with what was happening as he licked her center and his fingers glided in and out of her. The pressure was intense. Building. Doubling. Rising. Cresting. And then the pleasure broke through an invisible barrier, crashing into her with unbelievable force. Sophie gasped and her head jerked forward as she rode out each wave. Jake stilled both his hand and mouth, but he didn't lose contact until she began to come down from her heavenly high.

She grasped both sides of his face, raising his lips

to hers and kissing him deeply. She felt as if she were floating in all that warmth and contentment. "That was unbelievable." She peppered his face with kisses, wanting him to know how much she appreciated his masterful effort. Reaching down with one hand, she took hold of his rock-hard length. She could feel the pressure beneath his smooth skin. He was just as turned on by pleasing her as she was by the idea of doing the same for him. "It's your turn. I want to make you feel good."

They switched places and she licked her lips in anticipation of taking him into her mouth. He surprised her by leaning forward for another soft and sensuous kiss. "You already make me feel good, hummingbird. And I can't wait for more."

Six

By Sunday afternoon, the snowplows had done their job. The roads had been cleared, which meant the Eden House caretaker had done the same for the private drive leading to what had become Jake and Sophie's weekend retreat. Their hiding place.

Standing in the foyer of Eden House, Jake dreaded saying goodbye. He didn't want to end things the way he needed to—neatly. He didn't want to hurt Sophie. Quite frankly, he couldn't afford to hurt her. He should have thought this through better, but he hadn't. He'd given in to desire when he knew he couldn't follow through and give her more. The professional relationship he hoped to form with her made his mistake markedly more complicated.

"I'd say thank you for the hospitality if it didn't feel so inadequate."

"It wasn't like I had a choice. You showed up on my doorstep in the middle of a blizzard. I couldn't make you sleep in your car."

Sophie leaned closer and jokingly elbowed him in the ribs, but he took the chance to pull her into his arms and steal what could very well end up being their last kiss. *One more.* He closed his eyes and breathed her in, wishing things were different. Wishing he was different. When their lips parted, Sophie had a blissful smile on her face, her eyes only half-open. She looked like an angel. Meanwhile, Jake felt like the devil. Guilt was crashing down on him like that doorstop on Sophie's foot.

"It really was an amazing weekend. Thank you." He had to ease into this. He had to find the right words.

"You're welcome."

"Take care of that foot, okay?"

"It's much better today, but I still think I'm going to have to wear something sensible to work tomorrow." She jutted out her lower lip, and for a flash, all he could think about was sweeping her back upstairs and taking off every shred of her clothes.

But no. He had to return to work. Back to reality and responsibilities. He had to go back to the version of himself who didn't give in on a whim, the man who did not throw caution to the wind. "You know, it might be better for both of us if we keep this quiet. You know how people talk, and there's already so much gossip going around with you and Mindy inheriting the store. I wouldn't want my business partners to find any of this suspicious."

Sophie smiled, but it was pained. "Of course. Makes perfect sense."

"Are you sure? I don't want you to tell me one thing when you're thinking another. It nearly cost us our friendship the first time."

She nodded and started leading him toward the door. "I'm absolutely sure. It's not a good idea, especially when you want one thing for my business and I want another."

"Technically that's true, but I'd still like to find a way to hold on to our friendship. It's important to me. Truly."

"I know. Me, too. Don't worry about it. I guess I'll talk to you sometime after my grandmother's will is read?"

Jake knew that was the most sensible course of action. So why did the very idea of staying apart make his stomach sour? "I don't think we have to stay that far apart. We could have lunch one day. Maybe dinner."

"We'll see. December is crazy for me. The store. Christmas."

It wasn't quite the answer he hoped for. He wanted her to participate in this mini-negotiation. He wanted her to stumble through the dark with him, and help them arrive at a set of parameters that kept their roles and expectations clear. "I get it. You're a very busy businesswoman. Lizzie told me so every time I called and you weren't available."

Sophie planted a final, parting kiss on his cheek, then thrust a tin of Christmas cookies into his hand. They'd ended up baking them at two in the morning. Sophie had been that insistent and determined. Before that, they'd been equally occupied with each other. "Here. Don't eat all of these on the ride home."

"I'll do my best."

Out into the cold, he trudged to his car. For the entire ride home, his final exchange with Sophie tumbled around in his head. For someone who truly didn't want to hurt her, he sure had a talent for leading them both into situations where that was likely. He decided that the house had given him a false sense of security. They'd been tucked away from the rest of the world, and repercussions had been a distant thought. And then there was Sophie—she was too much for him to handle. He had to resign himself to this. She was the one woman who made him question his plans, both personally and professionally.

Very little was any clearer the next morning as he arrived at his office. He did know that it had been less than twenty-four hours away from Sophie and the notion of returning to work felt like a burden. All he really wanted to do was see her, or at least talk to her. He wanted to know that everything was okay between them. Could they remain friends after their weekend? Was that what she wanted? Or did she want more? Judging by her reaction when they'd parted, she was happy with the way things had ended. But Sophie had concealed her true feelings before. Was she doing it again? And if he managed to get through to her true feelings, could he live with the answer? Either she was fine with the noncommittal goodbye, which meant he hadn't left a mark on her the way she'd left one on him. Or if she wasn't okay with it, well, he'd gone and hurt her again. How could he have allowed himself to repeat the same mistake?

His email inbox was no help in trying to think less about Sophie. His voice mail wasn't much better. He had messages from each of his fellow members of the War Chest. They all wanted to know about Eden's and whether or not he'd been successful convincing Sophie. Yes, he'd made inroads, but not the sort of steps forward anyone had any business knowing about.

As he listened to voice mails, he wished he had more time to devise a different plan. Could he liquidate enough assets and make the Eden's purchase on his own? Or perhaps try to become her business partner? He'd done his research on the store. He knew where she could succeed and where she might fail.

Jake's assistant buzzed him. "Mr. Wheeler, Sawyer Locke is on the phone for you."

Sawyer was not only Jake's closest friend in the War Chest, he was one of the few real-estate developers in the city Jake enjoyed spending time with socially. "Sawyer. What are you up to?"

"Oh, you know. The usual. Happy to be back at

the office after a weekend of changing diapers and getting almost no sleep."

"Sounds like fun." Jake laughed, although his own reality was so far from Sawyer's that he could hardly imagine it. Sawyer and his wife, Kendall, had a baby at home, a little girl named Violet, if memory served.

"Actually, it is fun. I love being a dad. But that's not why I called. You know I have to ask about your meeting with Sophie Eden. Did it actually happen?"

"It did. We talked quite a lot, actually."

"And so? What happened?"

Jake wasn't sure how he should respond. He was *not* about to kiss and tell. It wouldn't reflect well on him and it wasn't fair to Sophie, either. The fact that he had to couch his answer only confirmed to him that he had, indeed, made a mistake. "We discussed the state of her business. I expressed our eagerness to do a deal, but in the end, we agreed not to discuss anything until her grandmother's will is read on December 18. Anything before that would be premature. She's still grieving and she wants to wait until everything can play out as her grandmother intended. I had to respect her wishes. She holds all the cards here."

The other end of the line was painfully quiet for what felt like an eternity. "I have to be honest, Jake. This makes me nervous. That's two weeks away. A lot could happen between now and then. You know as well as I do that Eden's has a lot of suitors. We're giving everyone else a chance, and I don't like it."

"She promised me that she wouldn't cut a deal with anyone without speaking to me first."

"She promised? Did you sign some sort of agreement?"

"I'd call it a handshake. I've known Sophie for a long time. I'm not worried about her sticking to a promise." Jake's stomach became more uneasy with every passing word. Would his initial plan to travel to Eden House and mend things with Sophie ultimately backfire?

"Okay, then." Sawyer's voice was pure exasperation. "I guess we have no choice but to trust your judgment. It still makes me nervous, though. This is a huge deal. I don't want us to miss out."

"I know. I know. I don't want us to lose it, either. Believe me, I'll do everything I can to keep that from happening." That much he could promise.

As soon as Jake hung up, his cell phone buzzed with a text. It was like Sophie knew that she was on his mind. Despite the tension of his conversation with Sawyer, it took only a few words from Sophie to put a smile on his face. What a pleasant surprise.

Work sucks.

He grabbed his phone and leaned back in his chair to type a response. It does.

I wish we were back at the house gorging ourselves on cookies.

All Jake could think about was what had happened after they'd done their baking, when Sophie started a powdered-sugar fight and they ended up making out in the kitchen. I wish we were doing the things we did after the cookies.

The blinking dots that meant Sophie was typing her response appeared on his screen. He waited expectantly, all the time wondering what must be going through her head. Was she feeling the same way he was? Or had he pushed it too far? Finally, he got a reply.

What are you doing tonight?

Bingo. Nothing. As in I'm available.

8:30? It's the earliest I can knock off.

Sure.

My place? Bring champagne?

What are we celebrating?

The end of the workday?

Good enough for me. See you then.

Audrey buzzed Jake's line, making him jump. "Sawyer Locke is on the line again."

Jake picked up, his body buzzing from his text exchange with Sophie. "Sawyer. Did we forget something?"

"I just got off the phone with my brother. He got his hands on some information about Eden's. If what he heard is true, we could be in big trouble."

Sophie was fairly sure she shouldn't have sent flirtatious texts to Jake, but she wanted to test the waters. Just because he'd said he wanted to keep things quiet didn't mean he wanted to *end* things between them. It had been her mistake to assume that yesterday morning. The old Sophie, the version of herself from eight years ago, jumped to conclusions like that. The more seasoned Sophie didn't want to. It gave Jake too much power. She could steer this ship as well as anyone. She just had to hope it didn't capsize because of her choices.

The promise of seeing Jake again made it nearly impossible to focus on work. All she really wanted to do was reread their texts and fantasize about what might happen at her apartment later tonight. She was assuming a lot, based on only a few words that they hadn't even spoken to each other, but she wanted to go on her gut with this one. Their weekend together had meant something. To both of them. She'd heard the genuine appreciation in Jake's goodbye, and she'd also felt his hesitation at leaving.

But what if she was wrong? What if he'd tricked her into thinking they could have more? She wanted to think she could be satisfied with only this second taste of Jake. She was so much stronger than she had been eight years ago. She had more confidence, was more resilient and self-assured. Even then, she doubted it in herself. She would be hurt if and when he called things off. Her marshmallow-like insides were still there, even if her outer shell had hardened.

As for what that meant for this Eden's deal that Jake was so desperate to make? The truth was that Sophie had only suggested they stop talking about it in order to give herself a break from saying no. It had conveniently come at a time when all she'd wanted to say to him was yes. Nothing about her plans for the future had changed. She would not sell the store. Not to Jake or anyone else who might come along. She would not let Gram's memory down. That was the top of her priority list, and she couldn't envision a reason why that would change. Not even the allure of pleasing Jake could make her set aside her family loyalty.

Sophie jumped when her cell rang and she saw Jake's name on the caller ID. Was he eager to chat? Was texting not enough? Or was he calling to cancel? The way her heart skipped and stumbled at the thought of each possibility should have told her that perhaps getting involved with Jake was not the wisest choice.

"Hey," she said. "This is a pleasant surprise."

"I have something I need to talk to you about."

"Oh. How nice." Just hearing Jake's voice made Sophie draw her finger along the edge of her desk and lazily lean back in her chair. Dreamy thoughts of what it was going to be like to see and touch him again flooded her brain. She could definitely get used to this feeling. "Do you want to wait so we can talk about it in person?"

"This can't wait. I'm calling because the word on the street is that there's another buyer in the mix for Eden's and I'm wondering what in the hell happened since I left Eden House yesterday."

Sophie sat up so fast her chair made a clunking noise. "Another buyer? What are you talking about?"

"Sam Blackwell. Wall Street guy. Real shark. He's going around telling people that the Eden sisters are in the palm of his hand. I thought I had the inside track here, Sophie. We agreed to that much. You wouldn't lead me astray on that, would you?"

What in the world had happened while Sophie was away? "Jake. I don't even know this Sam Blackwell person, so he must have talked to Mindy. You do have the inside track. I told you that. But it's the inside track on nothing right now. I've been nothing but incredibly clear with you. I'm not ready to sell. I might never be ready to sell."

Jake grumbled. "You can't mess around with him, Sophie. Sam Blackwell is a player and he will not hesitate to resort to dirty tricks to get what he wants. We're talking employee tampering or choking off supply lines to kill your business. He has connections with the city that are downright scary. If there's a single thing out of whack with your deed to that building or the property, you could lose it."

Sophie's heart was pounding so fiercely she was afraid she might be having a heart attack. Was there really someone out there powerful enough to take the store away from her? "How could someone do that? It doesn't seem possible. I'll talk to our lawyers. I won't let it happen."

"That's not a bad idea. But first, you need to shut down Sam Blackwell. You need to let him know you have no interest in doing business with him."

"Are you making this suggestion as my friend or as the person who wants to be victorious when this is all said and done?" Sophie hated that she had to question his motives. Jake made no secret of how competitive he was with other investors, especially other men.

"Both. Either. I'm both of those people. I do care about you, Sophie. I don't want you to get ripped off or mixed up with the wrong guy."

Sophie sighed and pinched her lower lip. Was that true? Did he really care about her? Or was this all about business?

Lizzie poked her head into Sophie's office. "I'm sorry to interrupt, but Mindy's on the line for you."

Speak of the devil. "Jake, my sister is on the other line. Let me go so I can talk to her. I have a sneaking suspicion she can shed some light on the Sam Blackwell situation. I'll let you know what she says. Like I said, this is the first I've heard about this."

"Perfect. Yes. Call me back."

"Will do."

Sophie hung up and, for a moment, stared at the phone on her desk. She hated feeling so out of the loop, especially on a matter of which she made up

50 percent of the vested interests. She really didn't like the fact that Jake had caught her so off guard. Why did she always have to be the last person to find out these things?

"Mindy. Hey. I need to talk to you," Sophie said when she picked up the extension.

"Are you back in the city?" Mindy replied, ignoring Sophie's request. "I was worried about you. Or should I say I was worried about you guys?" A mischievous snicker followed the question. "How is Jake, anyway?"

"I got back last night. And it's not like we were in danger. You know that. It was just some snow and bad roads. It was all clear by yesterday afternoon."

"How did things go? Between you and Jake? Was it like old times? Or did he just want to twist the thumbscrews on Eden's?"

Any number of interactions could fall under the purview of old times for Jake and her—everything from hanging out like buddies to falling into bed. She was thankful the latter had happened, at least to know now that Jake was genuinely attracted to her. That wasn't the reason he called things off all those years ago. Something else had been at play, most likely a case of twentysomething male jitters. "It was nice. We have definitely rekindled our friendship, which is great." Sophie decided to stop at that. She wanted to keep some things to herself.

"Did you talk about Eden's at all? Because I have something I want to discuss with you."

"Jake told me there's another buyer in the mix?

He's not happy about it, and quite frankly, neither am I. It's one thing to talk to Jake, and it's quite another to bring someone else in. Starting a bidding war doesn't do any good when I haven't agreed to sell in the first place. You're just going to end up making people mad."

"Will you slow down? I didn't plan for this to happen. It just happened. The guy's name is Sam Blackwell. I was out with some friends at a bar Saturday night and he approached me. He's a Wall Street guy. He does some real-estate investments, but it's not the only thing he does."

"Jake told me who he is. He hates him. He says he's a total snake. I can't believe you let some guy chat you up in a bar without first finding out who he was."

"Well, he is incredibly handsome. Who was I to send away a good-looking guy who wants to buy me a drink? And that's all it was. A Manhattan and a conversation. Perfectly innocent."

"From everything Jake said, there's nothing innocent about this guy at all. I don't like the idea of a person like this being within fifty feet of our grandmother's store."

"Hold on a second. Are you mad because I spoke to someone about selling the store and property or are you mad because that someone wasn't Jake? Did you two cut a deal over the weekend? Without me?"

"In fact, we agreed to the opposite. No talking about it until after the will is read. I can't believe you're even suggesting it."

"How am I supposed to know what went on between you two when you were stuck in that big beautiful house with nothing but a fully stocked wine cellar, a roaring fire and complete privacy?"

"Now what are you suggesting? That Jake and I are involved? Because we aren't." Were they? Her text conversation with Jake sure made her think they might be. Sophie buried her head in one hand, holding the phone to her other ear. Right now, she needed Mindy her sister, not Mindy her business partner. "At least I don't think we are."

"Sounds to me like somebody is confused."

"That's just Jake. He has that effect on me."

"Even after all this time? You need to get a grip, Soph. He's just a man."

Just a man. Easy for Mindy to say. She wasn't a hopeless romantic like Sophie. She didn't have a bad habit of holding out hope forever, like Sophie did. "Do you really not know what it's like when somebody has your number? When a guy could walk into the room for the five hundredth time and you're still just as bowled over by him as you were the first time you saw him?"

"No. I do not put men on a pedestal. If a guy is hot, he's hot. I don't sit there and think about how hot he is. I just go up and talk to him if I'm interested."

Yet more evidence that perhaps Mindy and Sophie should get their DNA tested someday. Sophie still wasn't sure they were truly related. "I don't put all men on a pedestal. Just some. And believe me, I would be much happier if he wasn't up there. It's just my stupid brain. I look at Jake and all I can see is everything I ever wanted." If that wasn't damning, Sophie didn't know what was. Jake's hold on her was just as strong now as it had been the first time. She needed to work harder at not giving him so much power.

"Wow. Seriously?"

Sophie sighed for what felt like the one hundredth time. "Yes. I can't help it. There's just something about him. Those green eyes and his mouth and the way he makes me laugh, especially at the most inopportune moments."

"Oh, my God. You really did sleep together."

Sophie's shoulders dropped. There was no point in hiding it. Mindy was smart. Sophie couldn't deny it forever. "We did." Sophie considered calling it inevitable, but it truly wasn't. Even when Jake had shown up at her door, even when she realized they were all alone, she never assumed he would want her.

"How was it?"

"Amazing. Completely incredible." Sophie didn't want to get too stuck in memories of her weekend with Jake, but everything was still so fresh in her mind—the way he smelled, the way it felt to be in his arms, the way it erased so much of the hurt and pain of the years spent apart. It was perfect. A little too perfect. Things with Jake and Sophie did not have a habit of working out.

"I want to be happy for you, Sophie, but this could put us at a huge disadvantage. Are you going to be able to say no to him if there's a higher bidder?"

"It's not a disadvantage because we're not selling."

"And I'm not running Eden's with you. Nor am I any less financially strapped than I was the last time we talked about this."

"You know I'm not in a position to buy you out."

"Again, you're making my case for me. If we sell, you won't have to worry about it. All of our problems will be solved."

Sophie needed to put an end to this discussion. Her head and her heart couldn't take running in circles with her sister, especially with Jake Wheeler walking around the world, able to pull at her strings. "Look. Nothing can be done until the will is read. Can we just put this entire discussion on a shelf until then?"

"Only if you'll promise we'll have a real discussion then. A real one where you remember that not everything is about what you want."

"And you need to promise that you will talk to Sam Blackwell and get him to keep his mouth shut. And I'd like you to remember for just a few minutes that you are a member of the Eden family."

"As if I could ever, ever forget."

Sophie got off the phone with her sister, but she wasn't ready to call Jake right away. She needed time to think about everything Mindy had said. Maybe Sophie did put men on a pedestal. Maybe she shouldn't let him know how willing she was to make him happy. It took away all of her power. She could learn at least that much from her sister.

Minutes ticked by on her phone. She waited for

ten, and then Sophie plucked it from her desk and dialed Jake's number.

"What did she say?" he answered right away, sounding desperate for anything but a romantic or flirtatious phone call with her.

"She said that he approached her in a bar and they had a drink. That was it."

"That's not what I'm hearing."

"I don't know what to tell you. That's what she told me. I don't tend to question my sister too much. She's never lied to me before and I don't think she has any reason to lie to me now."

"Okay."

"You don't sound convinced."

"I'm not, but I don't know what else I can do about it."

"Well, think of it this way. Nothing can happen without me, and I promised you that I will not agree to a single thing pertaining to the ownership of Eden's without first telling you."

"I know. And I appreciate that."

"That doesn't mean I'm going to sell to you. But it does mean that you'll know as much as I do."

"That's all I need for now."

Sophie couldn't help but feel once again that Jake was holding all the cards and she was holding none. How did she end up feeling this way? She was the one who owned half of a $4 billion property, after all. She wasn't without resources. "Well, good. Guess I'd better get back to work."

"Me, too. I'm swamped. In fact…" Ominous silence came from the other end of the line. "I don't think tonight is going to work. I'm sorry. I'm still catching up from being away on Friday."

Sophie pressed her lips together hard, fighting back the crush of disappointment. "I'm too busy, too." She *was* too busy. But she would have found a way to see him. She would have.

"Maybe tomorrow?"

"We'll see." She didn't want to play games. She was simply having a hard time keeping it together.

"Okay, then."

Sophie hung up, immediately launching into a lecture to herself. *Don't be sad. He's busy. You're busy. You can't live and die by his approval or how much he chooses to make himself available. You do your thing. He'll do his. And what happens, happens. Be a little more Mindy, and a little less Sophie.*

These were all apt and good words for her to internalize, but the truth was that as unsure as she'd been of Jake's motives over the last few weeks, she felt that doubly now. The instant there was even a glimmer of bad news, a small chance that he might not get his deal, he was no longer fun-and-flirty Jake. He was incredibly busy, noncommittal Jake. Well, two could play at that game.

Sophie got up from her desk, marched to the elevator and meandered through the store, talking with some of her salespeople and making sure everyone was happy and, most important, full of the Christmas spirit. She helped men choose cashmere gloves for their wives and girlfriends. She helped an elderly woman onto the escalator and accompanied her to housewares to find a set of pots and pans for her niece. She scooped up a young boy who was running through lingerie screaming at the top of his lungs—his mother was relieved someone had found him. With a reassuring pat on the back, she offered him a candy cane from behind the register and wished them both a merry Christmas. She did everything Gram would have done if she was feeling lost and unsure of what to do next. Sophie clung to the one thing she knew she could count on—the magic of Eden's, especially at Christmas.

It was past eight when she decided to head back to her office. Her foot, still not fully healed, was aching, and so was her pride. She hated that she was so disappointed she wouldn't see Jake tonight. As she walked among the flocked trees and life-size nutcrackers, the giant candy canes and swags of pine with wide velvet ribbon, she couldn't help but wonder what made him dislike these things so much. She wished Jake could see the world the way she did—mostly full of good things and good people. For her, Christmas was a reminder of those things, a time to take stock and be thankful. If only Jake loved it like she did, he might open his eyes and see that a woman who would love to have a chance with him was sitting right under his nose.

Seven

Jake hadn't talked to Sophie in two days, and it was eating away at him more and more with every passing minute. He hated the way they'd left things the other day. He didn't enjoy being the guy who doesn't trust, but that was exactly who he was. The mere idea of another buyer in the mix, the thought that Sophie might have gone back on her word, had made him so anxious he was practically sick.

That reaction was ingrained, planted in his childhood when the two people he counted on more than anyone, his mother and grandmother, had betrayed him. His mother by making an empty promise to find them a better life and come back for him. His grandmother by never extending a single loving or caring gesture, made all the worse when it was clear that Jake's mom would never return. Any hope of hugs and *I love you* were gone by then, replaced by reprimands and a never-ending guilt trip. He was a burden—a mouth to feed and more laundry to wash. He was no longer a boy. He was a creature. He was something to be tolerated, and he felt the shame and betrayal to this day. He'd learned to live with it, but it would always be there.

That was why he doubted his ability to live up to what Sophie wanted, needed and deserved. No matter how much he'd learned to ignore his scars, the aftershocks still turned up. Every time he made a knee-jerk reaction to feeling deceived or misled, he knew it had all started when he was a kid.

Still, he didn't want to make excuses for himself. His past might have made him skittish when he was younger, but he was thirty-two. He had to get his act together, and there was only one woman he could imagine doing that with—Sophie. If he wanted any chance at having a future that went beyond work, work and more work, he had to make things better with Sophie, even when the news of a second buyer for Eden's had knocked him back on his heels.

He was going to start with her assistant.

"Sophie Eden's office. This is Lizzie."

"Lizzie. Hi. It's Jake Wheeler." Jake rose from his desk and closed his office door. Audrey was a fantastic assistant, but she was nosy, and if she learned that his previous attempts to get Sophie's attention had turned into a romance, he'd never hear the end of it.

"Mr. Wheeler. Ms. Eden is on a call right now."

"Actually, I need to talk to you for a minute."

"Ms. Eden has instructed me to put you through if you're on the line. If you want to wait a moment, I can get her."

Jake grinned. This was the glimmer of hope he'd needed. Sophie had called off the guards at some point. Maybe not today or yesterday, but she'd still done it. "No, Lizzie, I don't think you're listening to me. I need to speak to you."

"Oh. Okay." She sounded genuinely surprised.

"Can you tell me when Sophie is leaving for the evening?"

"She'll be here until the store closes at ten. Possibly later. She works that late every night these days."

Poor Sophie. She worked longer hours than anyone he knew. "What about dinner? She has to eat."

"I typically order in for her and she eats at her desk around eight. She's having sushi tonight."

"Perfect. Can you tell me where you're ordering from and I'll pick it up?"

"I'm sorry, Mr. Wheeler. I'm confused."

"I just want to surprise her. I have a few things to apologize for."

As requested, Lizzie shared the information about Sophie's take-out order. Jake had Audrey pick up a bottle of Krug and put it on ice. He left the office at seven fifteen and arrived at Eden's, dinner in tow, just as Lizzie was packing up her things at her desk.

"Heading out for the night?" he asked Lizzie, craning his neck to see if he could catch a glimpse of Sophie, but her office door was closed.

"I am. I thought I was going to have to buzz you up. How'd you get past security?"

"I made friends with Duane. He's a real teddy bear when you get to know him."

Lizzie laughed. "It's sweet of you to bring her dinner. She's been so stressed. It'll be good for her to have a break."

"Exactly my thinking." Jake headed back to Sophie's office and knocked softly.

"Come in," she called from inside.

He opened the door, but Sophie was practically impossible to see. A mountain of paperwork sat on her desk. "Hello?"

From behind all that paper, Sophie's head popped up. "Jake? What are you doing here?"

The second he set eyes on her, a huge grin sprang up on his face. He couldn't have hid it if he tried. God, he'd missed everything about her—her voice, the sweet smell that filled her office. Her presence and spirit. "Hey there." He held up the take-out bag and the bottle of champagne. "I brought dinner. And something to help you relax."

Sophie rounded her desk in a red dress. He was immediately fond of the deep neckline. It showed off her cleavage in a way that left his body buzzing. "I thought you were swamped. I thought you were too busy for socializing." Suddenly her voice was clipped and cold.

"I was. But now I'm not. And this is my peace offering, too."

"I wasn't aware we were at war."

"Let's just say I'm not overly proud of the way I acted when the Sam Blackwell news popped up. I'm sorry. Very sorry."

She drew in a breath so deep her shoulders bunched up around her ears. "I would never lie to you, Jake. If you don't believe that, I can't spend time with you."

He nodded. Sophie was the exact test he needed. Although he was off to a slightly bumpy start, this had been the right thing to do. "I know that. I do."

"Thank you for saying you're sorry. I appreciate it." She reached for the bottle of champagne. "Apology accepted. Now let's break into this bad boy. I've had the worst day. I'll go find us some glasses."

Deeply relieved, Jake took off his coat and set out their meal on the coffee table in her office, which sat in front of a long velvety gray sofa. He took the liberty of flipping off the harsh overhead fluorescent lights and instead turning on two floor lamps on either end of the sofa. It gave the room a much softer and admittedly more romantic feel.

Sophie returned with a pair of coffee mugs. "Sorry. This is all I could find. We have real glassware somewhere, but only Lizzie knows where everything is." She padded over to him and sat.

"You're barefoot. That's not really your look."

Sophie did the honors with the champagne this time. "It isn't, but flats are surprisingly uncomfortable and my foot still isn't one hundred percent. Hopefully I'll be back in heels by tomorrow." She held up her mug and clinked it with his.

"To good friends who will accept apologies," he said.

"To good friends who show up with unexpected surprises."

They each took a sip, neither taking their eyes off the other. If Jake wasn't mistaken, the electricity was still here between them. The last two days hadn't cooled things off at all. Still, he knew he'd stupidly wasted that time. He should have been bringing Sophie dinner every night. He should have been bringing her lunch, too.

"I'm honestly surprised you aren't more annoyed with me than you are."

"I wasn't happy with you when I hung up the phone that day, but I thought about it and realized that was silly. You're a businessman. I'm not going to fault you for wanting to make sure you were getting your fair shake. You're also busy. I'm busy. These are just facts." She took a piece of sushi with chopsticks and popped it into her mouth.

"I should have given you the benefit of the doubt. I'm still sorry I jumped to the wrong conclusion."

Sophie dabbed at her lips with the napkin. "We've known each other for too long and we both work too hard to dwell on one conversation that didn't go great."

"Judging by your desk, I'd say you're really working too hard."

She glanced at the pile of papers threatening to topple onto the floor and shook her head. "It's ridiculous. I'm trying to analyze our sales and figure out where we can make some changes, but it's such a jumble. I should probably bring in a consultant, but I'll be honest. I don't want to spend the money."

Jake knew he could help her make sense of it. Perhaps not to the degree that an experienced retail consultant might be able to, but he could help. "I might have some insight."

"You don't strike me as a big shopper."

"I'm not. But I did a lot of research when my fellow investors and I decided to approach you and Mindy about purchasing the store. I might be able to help."

Sophie crossed her arms and sat back against the sofa cushions, her eyes full of skepticism. "Why would you do that? It's in your best interest if I fail."

He didn't have a rational answer to the question. What he wanted to do had no logical purpose in the scheme of his professional life. He was thinking with his heart and a few other body parts right now, not his brain. "I'd like to think it's in my best interest to make you happy."

Sophie stared at Jake for a possibly unreasonable amount of time, while her body was humming from what he'd said. "You want me to be happy?"

"I do. It's a beautiful thing to see." He took another slug of champagne from the coffee mug and cleared his throat. "Why don't you show me what you're looking at?"

Sophie went to her desk and gathered several binders of spreadsheets—detailed sales records spanning the last five years and projections based on the trends. In general, the news was not good. She brought them over to Jake and they spread them out on the coffee table.

He rolled his shoulders out of his suit jacket and tossed it over a chair. "Guess I'd better get comfortable if we're going to get to work." He began to roll up his shirtsleeves. Firm and taut with the perfect amount of dark hair, his forearms were crazy sexy, probably because she knew where they led—to his shoulders. And then to his chest, and eventually every other inch of his extraordinary body. "Do you want me to turn the lights back on? I went for mood lighting for dinner."

Sophie shook her head and scooted closer to him on the couch, stealing this chance to breathe in his warm scent. "No. I hate those things. This is much better."

They sat nearly shoulder to shoulder as Sophie walked him through the somewhat grim picture of Eden's Department Store. Unfortunately, the deeper she dug, the more she realized that Gram had made some poor decisions along the way, like not recognizing the importance of an online presence and putting enough money into a website.

"Everything I've read has just confirmed my suspicions," Jake said. "I'll be honest. This doesn't look great. But I have some ideas."

He then proceeded to dazzle her with about a dozen amazing concepts for changes she could make. Some were short-term fixes; others were long-term strategies. One involved nearly doubling the size of the women's shoe department and making Eden's online a true destination for female shoe aficionados everywhere, not just those who could make it to the store in New York.

"I'd be lying if I said that this idea isn't incredibly appealing to me."

"You do love your shoes."

She looked at him and smiled. "Thank you."

"For this? It's nothing. Just a few things I happened to notice while doing my due diligence." He waved it off and placed his arm across the back of the sofa.

Much like the moment at Eden House when they were in the sitting room and he'd taken the same pose, all she could do was think about kissing him. The only difference now was that she had the luxury of being less conflicted over it. "It's not nothing. There's a chance you just sank a billion-dollar deal."

"What's money when you have friends?" There it was—that extralow rumble of his voice that shook her to her core. In the soft light of the room, his eyes were dark and intense. "You are my friend, aren't you?" He trailed his hand up and down Sophie's bare arm, sending ribbons of electricity through her body.

With zero hesitation, she grasped his shoulder and shifted herself up onto her knees. "I'm whatever you want me to be, Jake." She leaned in, kissing him seductively so there could be no mistaking what she wanted. Him. Now. In her office. Lock the door. Things were about to get serious.

He returned the kiss, reining her into his arms and leaning back. Sophie hitched up her skirt and straddled his lap, resting her arms on his shoulders and digging both hands into his hair. Between her legs, heat blazed and Jake got hard—she felt it all even through layers of clothes. She ground her center against his length, wanting only one reaction from him, another of those sexy groans. When he made that exact noise, she laughed between their lips.

"What's so funny?" he asked, gathering her hair in his hands and kissing her neck.

"I just love it when you do that."

"Yeah?" He nuzzled his nose in the tender spot right below her ear. She drew her knees tighter against his hips, gripping his legs with hers.

"Yes. It makes me want you even more."

"Want to hear some good news? I have a condom in my wallet."

Sophie hummed in his ear. "Sounds like Christmas came early." She eased off his lap and let him reach into his pocket while she checked the outer office for employees. Thankfully, no one was around, but for privacy, she locked the door. When she turned around, Jake already had his shirt off and was standing there barefoot in his suit trousers.

Anticipation made her feel like she was flying as she rushed over to him. She stole a quick kiss while unbuttoning his pants and pushing them to the floor. She wrapped her fingers around him, stroking softly while she pressed her chin into his chest and gazed up at him. Full lips, stubble and the most intense eyes she'd ever seen, Jake was too handsome for words. He leaned down and kissed her, drawing down the zipper of her dress.

"I want you, Soph." His chest was heaving, his voice low and insistent.

"I want you, too." Not poetry, but it was all that came to mind.

He handed her the condom packet and she opened it, rolling it on him. He pulled her dress forward from her shoulders and it fell to the floor in a poof. Then they were in each other's arms, pressed tightly against each other, tongues mingling as they kissed and hands roved everywhere. Sophie was so overcome with want and need, she didn't know which way was up. Jake reached down and grabbed her bottom with both hands, lifting her up until she wrapped her legs around his waist. He plopped her down on the edge of her desk, right where all of those binders had been hours ago. This was going to be way more fun than work.

Jake grabbed one of her legs behind the knee and raised it to his hip. With his other hand, he moved himself inside her. Sophie rolled her neck, taking in the sensations. He was so hot. He was so perfect. She scooted herself to the very edge, grabbing on to him with both legs. Jake took deep thrusts while he lowered his head and drew her nipple into his mouth, rolling it gently between his teeth and giving it a tug. A flash of white zipped through her, leaving tension and heat between her legs. He was already on the brink. The pressure radiated from his hips and she felt it in his firm shoulders when she reached up to pull herself closer.

Her breaths were jagged. She couldn't draw in enough air. She was right on the edge, but she couldn't get there. She could feel the outer limits of her destination, but it was just out of reach. "I'm close, Jake. Keep going. Harder."

He was nothing but sheer determination, his fingers digging into the flesh of her bottom as his hips forcefully met hers. That was all she needed to tumble over the cliff and float off into bliss. She closed her eyes and gripped his shoulders as he reached his own climax, feeling more than merely physically gratified. There was an enormous sense of joy and relief that came with this moment. Jake had come back to her.

They both were still struggling for breath, clinging to each other. Sophie had her cheek flat against Jake's chest, but he lifted her chin with his finger and placed a soft kiss on her lips. "Remind me to visit you at work more often," he said, a smile spreading across his face.

"I'm glad I moved those binders. Now let's go sit on the sofa where we can be a bit more comfortable."

They parted for a moment, Jake cleaning up with some tissues he'd grabbed from the table next to her office door. He pulled on his boxer briefs, but left it at that, which Sophie loved. It was her favorite view.

From the end of the couch, she grabbed a throw blanket she used for late nights at the office. Still naked, she wedged herself between the sofa arm and

Jake, draping her legs across his lap and covering them both with the blanket. She wanted to be able to see his face when she talked to him. She needed that connection.

"I've always been curious where you got this." She smoothed her thumb over the scar above his eyebrow, her knuckles resting on his cheek. She'd never asked about it before. Jake was not forthcoming about himself or his past. She'd learned by now that if she did bring up a question like this, he would change the subject. But something about this moment made her want to take the chance anyway.

He grumbled and pulled her closer. "It's from when I was a kid." He trailed his fingers up and down her spine. If this was his way of distracting or deflecting, she might have to think of more potentially uncomfortable questions to ask him.

"But what happened?"

"Just an accident. It was nothing."

There was an edge to his voice that made her think there was more to it. Deep down, she wanted nothing more than to know more about Jake. He knew so much about her, had been fully pulled into her life from time to time. He knew her sister. He'd even met her mom at business school graduation. She knew next to nothing about him. "Was this when you lived in San Diego? What kind of accident?"

"Skateboard. I got off balance and went flying into a metal railing. I was just a stupid kid goofing around with his friends. It really wasn't that big of a deal."

She knew enough not to ask any more about the scar. "Did you skateboard a lot? Is that what you were into when you were younger?"

"Most kids in San Diego either skateboard or surf. It's just a Southern California thing. I wasn't anything special."

She scanned his face for some sign of what he was feeling, of why he was getting so on edge about this subject. "I'm sure you were all kinds of special."

"You're the one who's special." He murmured the words into her hair, his arm around her tight. "I don't think I should leave tonight without us making a real plan to see each other. I was thinking maybe even a date."

Sophie set aside her disappointment over his deflecting about his past. She could hardly believe what she was hearing. "I thought you wanted to keep things under your hat."

"That was a stupid suggestion. Especially since it was keeping me away from you. I don't care what people say or think."

Sophie didn't want to get too carried away, but she loved that he wanted to be a little reckless because of her. "What did you have in mind?"

"Whatever you want. Something fun."

Of course, in December, everything Sophie wanted to do in the city revolved around Christmas. Maybe this could be another chance to chip away at his grumpy holiday attitude and help him see the joy and merriment through her eyes. "I haven't been to the

Holiday Market at Bryant Park yet this year. I love going. I usually end up buying a ton of gifts."

Jake laughed. "With all of the amazing restaurants, bars and theater productions in the city, you want to go to that?"

"Yes. It's fun." She sat back and eyed him. "Have you been?"

"I haven't, but I can see it from the windows of my office. I see it every day right now."

She sensed that he wasn't thrilled about the prospect, but she decided to ignore that. She'd have to prove to him that they could have fun doing something he would normally avoid. "Then perfect. I'll scoop you up from work tomorrow night and I'll show you what you've been missing."

"I already know what I've been missing." He kissed her shoulder and caressed her arm softly. "I missed you, Soph. Is that crazy? After only two days?"

Goose bumps raced over the surface of her skin. She'd missed him, too. So much. "It's not crazy. At all."

Eight

Jake's plan for the Holiday Market was to indulge Sophie for an hour or two. He'd let her work out her Christmas urges—retail therapy or whatever they called it. Then he would whisk her away to his penthouse apartment, open a bottle of incredible wine, feed her a fabulous meal and, if all was right, take her to bed. The tryst in her office had been super hot, but he didn't want her to think a quickie on a desk was all he was after. Sophie deserved a soft bed and fine bedding. She deserved the luxury of a man who would take his time with her, which was precisely what he intended to do.

He was busy answering an email when Audrey buzzed the line in his office. "Mr. Wheeler, Ms. Eden is here."

Jake sprang from his desk chair like it was the ejector seat in a fighter jet. "Great. Send her in."

"Knock, knock." Sophie appeared in his doorway, grinning, wearing a light gray wool coat that was cinched in at the waist and flared out to her knees. Her beautiful red hair peeked out from beneath a white hat with an enormous fluffy pom-pom on top. She was…well, there weren't really words. Her face was one he wanted to look at forever. Sheer perfection. He was transfixed.

"Don't you look wintery? And gorgeous?" He tugged her into his arms and kissed her softly. It felt like the best reward after a long day at work. He could get used to this—seeing her every day. Being with her.

"We're going to be outside for hours. Despite my devotion to fashion, I have to stay warm." She stepped back and turned in a circle. "Look. Pants. And boots. I'm practically ready to take a dogsled into the Arctic."

"I see you couldn't give up on the heels."

She looked down at her feet, seeming nothing less than enormously pleased with her shoes. "Some compromises simply aren't worth making."

"Very chic. I love it." *I love you.* The words nearly tumbled out of his mouth. He had to steel himself for a moment, holding on to her shoulder for support.

Sophie's sights narrowed on him, brows furrowed. "Are you okay?"

Was he? With no earthly idea where those words had come from, he was inclined to think no. "Of course. Just admiring you. That's all." He leaned closer and kissed her cheek. "I'll get my coat."

As he threaded his arms into his black wool coat, he gathered himself, thankful he hadn't slipped and uttered those three little words. Yes, he cared about Sophie, but their relationship was all about small steps. There would be no leaps. *I love you* was months off. Maybe a year. And who knew if he and Sophie would even last that long? Right now, he was trying to simply enjoy every moment when he wasn't stricken with panic. He was savoring every instance when he didn't have the urge to run for the door.

But he couldn't deny that there had been a shift in his thinking over the past several days. First he'd missed her greatly, more than he'd ever missed anyone. Then there had been his immense relief that she was the sort of person simply willing to talk out a problem. She was willing to forgive him for having been less than pleasant. She was willing to forget those two days when he hadn't called. He not only hadn't experienced that in any relationship, he wasn't sure he was capable of the same thing. When you learn to hold on to someone else's mistakes, it's a hard habit to break.

But he was ready to be better than all of that. There was a lot at stake between Sophie and him, and it wasn't just a multibillion-dollar real-estate deal. The conversation in her office last night, the one that took place before clothes started to come off, had been extremely gratifying. She eagerly accepted his advice and insight, offering her own experience and taking his ideas to the next level. They'd fed off each other's enthusiasm to create a vision. It was the first time he'd thought that Eden's might actually succeed with Sophie at the helm. Yes, that threatened his potential big deal, but at this point, he had to be realistic. Sophie's devotion to Eden's wasn't going anywhere. In the end, it would likely all come down to practicality, money and the question of whether or not she could find common ground with her sister. He might need to do what he never did and leave that one up to fate.

"Ready?" he asked.

She popped up onto her toes like a cork out of a bottle of champagne. "Yes. I'm so excited."

"Let's go."

Hand in hand, they marched out of his office, past Audrey, who was packing up her things for the day. "Have fun," she called. Knowing her, she'd pepper him with questions tomorrow morning. He had to prepare for that.

They took the elevator down to the lobby and walked out into the brisk night air. Across the street, rows of glass and metal vendor kiosks ran along the terraces of the park. Even he had to admit the tiny buildings were enticing. Lit up, they each looked like a jewel box. Once they crossed over into this Christmas wonderland, it was hard not to get caught up in Sophie's sheer excitement.

"What do you want to do first?" Her cheeks were already bright pink, her eyes startlingly clear and bright. "We could get something to eat. They have these amazing Belgian waffles with little sugar pearls inside them."

"I thought you wanted to do some shopping." He squeezed her hand a little tighter.

"I do. If that's okay."

"Tonight is all about you. Lead the way."

And so she did, pulling him along until they arrived at a shop that mixed custom perfumes. "I got this for Mindy two years ago and she loved it. I want to do it again." Inside, the saleswoman and Sophie discussed her sister's personal preferences. Apparently she favored citrus over floral and sweet over woody notes. To Jake, it was all like a foreign language, but in the end, the pair concocted a fragrance that was surprisingly lovely. Jake was simply amazed at how much thought and care Sophie would put into a single gift. He had to wonder if Mindy knew how tuned in her sister was to what she wanted.

From there, they shopped for locally made handknit scarves, hammered silver earrings from Central America and women's silky robes made in India and trimmed in wide, embroidered sari ribbons. Jake was happily loaded down with the shopping bags. Watching Sophie enjoy herself made it all worth it.

"One more stop," Sophie said. "Then we can grab something hot to drink and watch the ice-skaters."

"Sounds like a plan."

She led him into a shop packed with people and stocked to the ceiling with every Christmas ornament you could imagine—jolly snowmen with stovepipe hats, glittery snowflakes, glass icicles and round-belly Santas hanging from metallic gold string. These were the trappings of Christmas that were most foreign to Jake. He knew they should make him feel happy and nostalgic, but he couldn't attach any meaning to them other than that they were the things he had missed out on.

"I always buy a new ornament every year. Gram did the same. She always bought hers at Eden's, but I think this place has a better selection."

"Remember that come next Christmas. You should be shopping at your own store and using what I'm guessing is a substantial employee discount." *Next Christmas*. Would Eden's still be there? Would he and Sophie last that long?

Sophie smiled and patted him on the chest, smoothing her hand up over his shoulder. Any worries about the future were quashed by the ripples of warmth she sent through him.

"You're so right," she said. "We need to step up our game for next year. We put so much effort into the stuff we don't sell, like the window displays and the decorations in each department."

"Well, that's an important part of it, too. People come to the store for the experience more than anything. You make them happy. That's what keeps them coming back."

She cocked her head and jutted out her lower lip. "That's so sweet. You're going to make me cry."

"Don't do that. You've been looking forward to this. You're having fun. Plus, I'm holding fifty pounds of Christmas gifts and could use a break. Let's get your ornament and get out of here."

Sophie made her selection—a happy snowman wearing a red stocking cap and sitting in a teacup. "What do you think?"

It was just as sweet and funny and unexpected as Sophie. "I think it's perfect."

Taking her place in line, she pointed to a gold star atop one of several Christmas trees displayed in the shop. "See that? That's what Gram's star looks like." Like many things at Eden House, the star was funky and unusual—1960s era possibly, with gold tinsel and glitter. "I still haven't heard back from Barry about finding the one up at the house." The corners of her mouth drew down, a sight he disliked so much.

"I'm sure it'll turn up. Who loses a Christmas star?"

And just like that, the frown was gone. "You're right. I shouldn't worry so much."

She paid for the ornament and they strolled to a coffee stand, where Jake ordered a latte and Sophie chose a hot cocoa with extra whipped cream. From there they wound their way to the ice rink at the opposite corner of the park. An older couple got up from a bench at the perfect time, and Jake was quick to snag it for them, setting down the bags and enjoying the chance to sit. He put his arm around her and watched the masses circling the rink. Holiday music filled the air, as did the sound of chatter, laughter and the occasional shriek when someone slipped and fell on the ice. Maybe it was just being with Sophie, but Jake was surprised to find that he was actually enjoying himself.

"This was nice. Thank you for bringing me."

Sophie removed the lid from her cocoa and swiped at the whipped cream with her tongue. Jake had to stare. It was too damn sexy. "Careful, Jake. Someone might notice you actually enjoying something related to Christmas."

"Hey. I'm not eager to return. This is exhausting. I don't know how you do it."

"I'm running on pure adrenaline these days. Trust me, I'll fall into a coma on December 26."

Jake laughed and pressed a kiss to her forehead. "I call that day Christmas Leave."

Sophie reared back her head. "Seriously?"

"Well, yeah. It's a joke. Like Christmas Eve, but it's the day after. Get it?"

"I get it. But I don't. It just seems so…"

"So what? Negative?"

"Yes. Exactly. And you aren't entirely like that. I've been watching you, Jake Wheeler, and you are not only capable of having a lot of fun, you also enjoy smiling and laughing and a million other pleasant things. So I still don't get what exactly it is about this holiday that makes you cringe."

Jake returned his sights to the ice rink for a moment, watching a young boy learning to skate with his mother's patient guidance. The little guy held his arms wide to brace his fall, but something about his stance said that he knew she would be there to catch him or, at the very least, pick him back up. The center of Jake's chest ached. There was a time when he would have done anything for five minutes of what that little boy had.

"You want to know the real reason I don't like Christmas?"

Sophie took his hand in hers, squeezing it tight. "Yes. I do."

Even with hundreds of people milling about, there was a stillness to the air around Sophie and Jake. She squeezed his hand a little tighter, studying his handsome profile. Even when he wasn't making eye contact, she sensed his vulnerability. Something deep and painful radiated from him. A part of her was scared to hear it, worried that it might change her vision of him as the strong and unflappable Jake. But a much bigger part of her simply wanted to understand the mystery. She wanted to see inside that head of his. She wanted to know the good, but she needed to hear the bad. "It's okay. You can tell me."

"I'm not the only one, you know. For a lot of people, Christmas is incredibly depressing."

"I know. I know it's hard on some people. But I want to know why it's hard on you."

"Where do I start? The commercialism. The running around for no good reason. The music is everywhere. Nobody gets anything done those last two weeks of the year. It's nothing more than a big disruption." He shook his head and looked down at his lap.

"That's an argument against celebrating. That

doesn't tell me what happened in your life that made you feel like this. Surely you loved Christmas when you were a kid. All kids love Christmas. You weren't born hating it. I know that much."

"Not all kids love Christmas."

The way he'd said it made Sophie's breath seize up in her chest. She'd known that getting Jake to open up would not be easy, but damn, he wasn't giving her much to work with. She had to keep pushing so she could understand what made him closed off sometimes. "Is that how you felt? As a kid?"

"I don't want you to think less of me. I don't want this to be what defines me." He turned and scanned her face, searching for something she desperately wanted to give him. If only he'd tell her.

She pulled him a little closer and kissed his cheek. "I will never think less of you. And the only thing that has to define you is your actions. You're more than your past. You're more than the bad things that have happened to you." Her brain whirred faster as she searched for the words that would get him to talk. "I'm sensing that you've never talked about this. And maybe that's why you're struggling. You've been carrying it around all this time. I think it might be good if you just let it go."

He swallowed so hard his Adam's apple bobbed up and down. "I don't know what I did to deserve having you come back into my life."

"Maybe I'm here because you need someone to listen."

He cracked just a fraction of a smile, but she

would take what she could get. "Maybe." He looked skyward at the midnight blue void hanging over the city. "Gram was everything to you, but my grandmother was a nightmare. And it was just the two of us from the age of seven. She was mean, she didn't want me around and she definitely did not believe in celebrating Christmas."

"How did you end up living with her?"

He refocused his sights on Sophie. "I never knew my dad. My mom got pregnant in high school, which infuriated my grandmother. I was just another mouth to feed. My grandmother worked during the day cleaning at a hotel. My mom didn't have anyone to take care of me, so she couldn't really get a job, but that just made my grandmother lash out at her. She'd tell her she was lazy. It was an impossible situation." Now that he was talking, he seemed calmer, but the words were coming faster, like he was rushing to get them out.

"Once I went to school, and got a little older and was able to take care of myself, my mom decided that was her chance to make a different life for us. She told me she was going to find a job and get us a place to live on her own, and that she'd come back for me. But she never came back. She left me with my grandmother. Forever."

Sophie was so still she had to hold her breath. "I had no idea all of that had happened to you."

"I don't tell anyone about it. I'm very good at hiding it."

"Too good." She shook her head. It just didn't seem real. "All I can think about is that day I met you and how you just seemed like such a golden boy to me. You were so handsome and sexy and oozing with confidence. It was mesmerizing."

"And largely an act." His gaze connected with hers again. "Well, not the handsome and sexy part. That part I come by honestly."

She laughed. "And the funny, self-deprecating, deflecting part. Don't forget that."

He smiled, which she loved seeing. It was such a bittersweet moment. "Never."

"Your scar. It's not from skateboarding, is it?"

He shook his head. "No. It's not. I forgot to take out the trash one day and my grandmother pushed me. I fell headfirst into the edge of a door."

Sophie gasped. Tears shimmered in her eyes at the thought of a young Jake at this woman's mercy. "I am so incredibly sorry."

"I don't want you to feel sorry for me, Soph. Please don't. Of all the things I want from you, pity isn't one of them."

Sophie desperately wanted to know what those other things were, but that was a question for another time. "It's not pity. I promise. But it hurts me to hear that those things happened to you. I hate it."

He shrugged. "It's just the way things played out. The reality is that those experiences are part of me, like anything else. And you know, I might not have become so successful without having that for motivation. I didn't want that life for myself. I worked my butt off in school and I moved as far away as I possibly could, as soon as I could, which is what brought me to the East Coast. If I hadn't done that, I might not have met you. My life would be very different now."

"That's such a nice way to think about it. I'm sorry I ever thought of you as a pessimist."

He shook his head. "Well, I am sort of a pessimist. Maybe fifty percent. I'm confident some things will work out. Just not everything. I can't be like you. I can't be all sunshine and rainbows."

Sophie could've denied it, but Jake never would have let her get away with it. "That's all Gram's influence. She always gravitated toward the light. I just try to follow that philosophy. If something makes you happy, if it makes you feel good, you should pursue it. Don't hold back."

A sweet smile spread across Jake's face. "Maybe that's why I'm so drawn to you. You're the light." He tucked a tendril of her hair back inside her hat. "I'm falling for you, Sophie."

"You are?" Sophie's heart jumped up into her throat. This was a revelation for which she had not prepared. She had a good handle on her own feelings, but not nearly enough of a good sense of Jake's. He always played everything so close to the vest. Not today, apparently.

He nodded. "I am. Hard. You make me happy. Happier than I've been in a long time. And you make me feel good." He pulled her closer, gazing down at her. "Will you let me make you feel good?"

Heat blazed in her cheeks and chest. Would his effect on her ever lessen? Or would it only continue to grow? She couldn't imagine what that would be like, but she wanted it more than anything. "You have a very special talent for making me feel good."

"Tonight, that's all I want to do."

Nine

Life with Jake had become a whirlwind. Ever since the night in her office, and especially since the Holiday Market, they'd been inseparable. There had been countless dinners and late-night rendezvous, visits to each other's offices and hours of talking in bed, in the dark, holding each other tight. With every passing minute together, Sophie fell a little further for him. The only question was whether he was traveling on the same path.

The reading of Gram's will today was going to complicate things. There was no question about that. A considerable chunk of Sophie's future would be laid out before her. The rest of it was all in Jake's hands. If he didn't want her, if he didn't feel the way she did, she wasn't sure she could muster much enthusiasm for anything, not even claiming her birthright, Eden's. They were going to have to revisit the discussion with Jake—the one she'd put on hold. It killed her to know that she was going to ultimately end up disappointing him. She didn't see another way. He would not get his big deal. He had to know that on some level. If he didn't, he was fooling himself. She just had to hope that, in the end, he would see that what they had between them was worth more than any money that might be made.

"Good morning," she whispered, curling into his naked chest and breathing in his smell. Like the last several nights, they had stayed over at his sumptuous penthouse apartment. Her place was really nice, but his was spectacular, high atop a skyscraper with the most stunning views of the city.

"Good morning, yourself," Jake mumbled, smoothing his hand around her bare hip and pulling her closer. "What time do we have to be at the lawyer's office?"

"Nine sharp. You know, you don't have to come with me if you don't want to. There could be drama with my mom. She and Gram never really got along, and I know for a fact that there were accounts that were supposed to go to my dad when Gram passed away. They never worked out what would happen with that money after my dad died. I'm worried my mom is counting on that money to survive."

"If you want me there, I want to be there for you. Plus, I'd like the chance to see Mindy and your mom.

I'm sure I'll be fine with whatever family drama happens to come up."

Sophie smiled and kissed him on the nose. "Good. Because I do want you there. I always want you by my side." She stopped herself from saying the words that were waiting on her lips—everything about not wanting him to walk away from her today. How she hoped that he would eventually find a way to go from falling for her to actually loving her. Because the truth was that Sophie loved him. She absolutely loved him. She'd loved him eight years ago, and she loved him even more now. As to when she could share that confession, she had no idea when that day would come. She couldn't bring herself to say it if she wasn't reasonably sure it would be returned.

"I'll put coffee on if you want to get into the shower," Jake said, glossing over the weight of what she'd just said about always wanting him by her side. It felt like confirmation that they were still operating with two separate sets of rules.

"Great." Sophie watched as he traipsed out of the room in only his pajama pants. She might as well soak up every beautiful view she could.

She showered and dressed in a chic but subdued black dress with a princess-seamed bodice and a full skirt. Today's shoes were anything but quiet, though—pale-pink-and-black patent-leather spectator pumps, courtesy of Mr. Blahnik's divine skills. Gram had always commented on them. That felt important today.

"Ready?" Jake asked as he walked into the kitchen still tying his tie.

"Yes. Come here." Sophie straightened the Windsor knot and neatened his collar. Jake was always put together, but even the most polished man needed help when he didn't have the benefit of a mirror. She watched as he pulled on his jacket and fastened the top button. "You look very handsome today." He really did. His charcoal-gray suit brought out his mesmerizing green eyes.

"You look spectacular. But you probably already know that."

"I promise you I will never tire of hearing it."

Hand in hand, they made their way down to the elevator and then to the garage, where Jake's driver was waiting for them. It was about twenty blocks downtown and a few avenues west to Gram's attorney's office, so it was a good thirty-minute trip in morning traffic. Sophie had considered softening the eventual blow of her decision to keep Eden's while they were in the car, but Jake got a phone call as soon as they got settled in the back seat. She calmed herself by taking his hand and clutching it firmly. She couldn't let him get away. Not again. She would just have to help him see that they were in love, and that was the most important thing.

When they pulled up outside the lawyer's office, Mindy was climbing out of a black stretch SUV. This was not her normal mode of transportation. Her car was much smaller and more modest. She'd often said she hated those big ostentatious cars. They felt snobbish to her.

"Did you get a ride from someone?" Sophie asked

when they met on the sidewalk. Jake had stepped inside the building vestibule, finishing up his phone call. Sophie tried to catch a glimpse of who was in the back seat, but the door had been closed too quickly for her to see.

"Oh. Just a friend." Mindy avoided eye contact, tugging at her red wool coat. Her normally tidy hair, a much darker shade of red than Sophie's, was anything but neat and polished this morning. Something was definitely up.

"What kind of friend?"

Mindy narrowed her stare, practically shooting daggers from her eyes. "Just a friend, okay? I don't want to talk about it."

Sophie kept quiet, but she couldn't help but notice how the skin around Mindy's mouth was red and her lipstick was only about half on. "Okay. I'm sorry."

Mindy stood a little straighter and cleared her throat. "You and I need to talk. Before we go in for the reading."

Sophie did not like that biting edge of her sister's voice. It sounded like bad news wrapped up in doom. She also didn't like being ordered around by Mindy. It was insulting. "Is something wrong?"

"I don't want to talk about it out on the street, okay?"

"Well, you could use a trip to the ladies' room to reapply your lipstick and fix your hair. Whatever you were doing with that friend you don't want to talk about has taken its toll." Sophie hustled inside and over to Jake, who put his hand over the phone receiver. "Mindy and I need to talk. I'll see you upstairs? It's Suite 401."

"Got it. I'll be done in two minutes."

"Sophie. Come on," Mindy said.

"I'm coming." She and Mindy rode the elevator to the fourth floor in silence. This building was filled to the brim with lawyers' offices and as old-school as it got, with speckled polished stone floors and glass mail chutes that were still being used on the rare occasion that someone needed to mail a letter.

The ladies' room was right off the elevator. Sophie led the way inside. Mindy checked under the stalls as the door swooshed shut. Sophie felt like they were in a spy movie.

When she'd completed her survey, Mindy turned to her. "We agreed that we wouldn't make any decisions until the will is read. So now that we're about to find out what we already know, I need to tell you that I've made a decision and you might not like it."

Great. Sophie's shoulders wanted to drop, but she wouldn't let them. She wouldn't let her sister beat her down like this. "Just tell me, Mindy. I'm tired of you holding everything over my head."

Mindy's jaw tensed. "Fine. Tomorrow, you're going to get a letter from my lawyer saying that you have six months to buy me out of my half of Eden's."

Sophie couldn't believe what she was hearing. She blinked again and again as if that would wash away the horror of it. "So that's it. No discussion. You're just going to have your lawyer settle this between us? You're my sister. I can't believe you would do this."

"You gave me no choice. You refused to listen to what I want and need for myself."

Sophie was filled with such disgust right now she could hardly see straight. "I swear, you are the most selfish person I have ever met. Our grandmother died and I'm doing everything I can to keep her dream alive, and you're fighting me every step of the way."

Mindy stepped closer. Her eyes were so angry it was as if they were on fire. "Are you listening to yourself? It was *her* dream, Sophie. And you feel a sense of obligation to see that through, but I don't. It might have been her dream, but it's not mine. My company is my dream. It's my vision. And I'm not going to take all of the hard work I've done to reach my goals and throw it away. I won't do it."

Sophie felt as though she couldn't breathe. Jake had warned her this might happen. He'd even told her to prepare herself for it, but she'd never believed that Mindy would be cold-blooded enough to do it. "So we're not going to work together. And I have to figure out how to buy you out of your stake in the business? We're talking two billion dollars for half of the current valuation, Mindy. Billion with a *b*. I don't have that kind of cash lying around. And I can't even begin to think where I'm going to get it."

"Then let me sell my half to Jake."

Sophie had thought about that once or twice, but she knew that wasn't what he was after. He and his partners wanted to buy the property so they could see Eden's to what they felt was its rightful demise. They wanted the building and the land. They envi-

sioned condos and big-chain retail and fancy restaurants. They would never go in on what they all saw
as a failing business. And Sophie wasn't willing to
give up. Not yet.

"I don't think that's going to work."

"Why not? Trouble in paradise?" Mindy stepped
up to the mirror and reapplied her lipstick, not ac-
knowledging the fact that she truly did look dishev-
eled.

"It's complicated."

"That's a Facebook status, not an answer."

Sophie simply stared at her sister's reflection in
the mirror. Some days it felt as though they would
never get along. It frustrated the hell out of her. Not
being able to count on Mindy only made Sophie realize that, aside from the loyal staff at Eden's, people
who were paid to be on her side, Jake was the only
person in her life who was truly supporting her. That
had always been Gram's role, and he'd filled it. For
that reason, she had to find him right now.

"Where are you going?" Mindy asked.

"To find Jake."

Jake was waiting in the hall outside the conference room where the will was to be read. A peculiar
edginess was in the air, which caught him off guard.
He hadn't expected to feel nervous today. This was
Sophie's day, and although it would be momentous,
it was supposed to be very straightforward. Everyone knew what was in Victoria Eden's will, at least
as it pertained to Eden's Department Store.

Still, Sophie and Mindy had been in the bathroom for a while now. He'd listened for the sound of arguing but hadn't heard a thing. That was a relief. By all accounts, there had already been more than enough tension between those two. When Sophie finally came strolling down the hall, he smiled at her, hoping that things would be okay between them after this was all over. He was fairly certain she wasn't going to be willing to sell him the Eden's property. They hadn't discussed it, but nothing about her dedication or hardworking attitude had changed. That meant that it would fall on him to break the news to his fellow investors. It wouldn't be easy. They might kick him out of the group. That would mean an entire stream of exclusive business opportunities, gone.

"They're ready for us," he said, kissing Sophie on the cheek. "Everything okay with Mindy?"

"Nothing two billion dollars can't fix," she quipped.

"You're kidding, right?"

She shook her head. "Afraid not."

A woman in a black suit stepped out of the conference room. "If we could get everyone situated inside, we'd like to start."

Sophie and Jake filed in behind her. Sophie came to a dead stop and grabbed his arm as soon as she stepped into the conference room.

"What?" Jake asked. "You okay?"

"My cousin Emma is here," she whispered, pulling Jake farther into the room, but into a corner away from the other people who had gathered. "So is my aunt Jill."

"So? I thought the whole reason the reading was delayed was because they had to wait for the beneficiaries to be here."

She squeezed his arm even harder and her eyes flashed with confusion. "But Emma is on the other side of the family. Her mom and my mom are sisters. Gram was my paternal grandmother. I didn't even know Gram knew Jill or Emma."

A team of lawyers was assembling at the head of the table. "Please. Everyone. Find a seat. We're going to start in a moment," the woman in the black suit said.

"I'm sure it's fine. Probably one of those things where they met her through your parents and she wanted to give them something to remember her by."

Sophie scanned Jake's face, her eyes darting back and forth. He could see the gears turning as she tried to make sense of what he was saying. "Okay. You're right. I'm sure it's nothing."

He took this moment of relative quiet to pull her closer. He drew the back of his hand across the smooth skin of her cheek. "It will all be okay. I promise."

He had to say something to reassure her. He couldn't stand to see her upset, even when his own stomach was churning. Talk about being torn—he wasn't sure how he would feel once the will had been read and Sophie, this beautiful woman he couldn't

get out of his system, had inherited the massive
Eden's business and property. Every moment with
Sophie was only pulling him closer to her.

"We'll go ahead and get started. I'm Leslie Adams
and I'm lead counsel for the Eden estate," the woman
said again. "If everyone could take a seat at the table,
that would be great."

Sophie and Jake stepped forward and each pulled
out a rolling chair. He sat on Sophie's left, and to Sophie's right, her mother, Jenny, took a seat. Mindy
walked in and took the seat next to Jake, mumbling a
quiet hello. Several of Sophie's grandmother's cous-
ins were next, followed by Emma, the mysterious
cousin, and Jill, the aunt. Jake could feel the tension in the air again, especially between Sophie and
Mindy's mom and her sister. They didn't even look
at each other.

Ms. Adams cleared her throat loudly, and that was
enough to garner everyone's attention. "This will be
a straightforward proceeding. The decedent, Victoria Jane Eden, asked that her last will and testament
be read aloud to her family." She then launched into
the legal preamble to the will, followed by a laundry list of antiques and jewelry, all of which went to
various family members. None of it seemed to war-
rant much of a response from those in attendance,
but perhaps that was because everyone was waiting
for the big-ticket items.

Ms. Adams turned a page of the will and re-
adjusted her reading glasses. "And finally, we move
on to the major assets." Everyone seemed to sit a little

straighter, bending their ears and hanging on every word. "'To my eldest granddaughter, Mindy Eden, I leave my apartment overlooking Central Park. I have had many happy years there and I hope she chooses to make it her permanent residence.'"

Mindy shifted in her seat, but made no indication as to whether or not she was happy about the news.

"'To my middle granddaughter, Sophie Eden, I leave Eden House, the family's vacation home outside the city limits of Scarsdale, New York. She loves the house even more than I do, and I know she will take good care of it.'"

Under the table, Sophie's hand found Jake's. She tugged on it hard. "Did you know that?" he whispered.

Sophie nodded. "Yes. But what does she mean middle granddaughter?"

There was no time to discuss it. The lawyer continued. "'And finally, the most important piece of my legacy, Eden's Department Store. The business and all its holdings, including the building and the property on which it stands, will go to my granddaughters, Mindy Eden, Sophie Eden and Emma Stewart.'"

There was an audible gasp in the room. Sophie's eyes flew back to Jake's, then over to Ms. Adams, who held a finger to her lips.

"Please allow me to continue." She looked down again and returned to the text. "'I promised my son, Mitchell, that I would not divulge this information, but now that he and I are both gone, I feel that the truth must come out. Emma is my granddaughter, the product of a brief dalliance between my son and his wife's sister, Jill Stewart. I was not proud that he had strayed, but that should in no way reflect poorly on Emma. She has spent her entire life caught up in an impossible situation. I felt it was only right for her to have her piece of my fortune, along with her half sisters.'"

You could have heard a pin drop in that room. Everyone was dead silent. Ms. Adams held up her finger. "'There is one stipulation to the ownership of Eden's, however. The three granddaughters must proceed in good faith to keep the store in business for two years by running the store together. If any of the three do not agree to this, they shall forfeit their share to the remaining heir or heirs, but the stipulation remains in place. The property and business may not be sold or handed over to any entity until after a period of two years. At that time, the three granddaughters must come to a mutual agreement regarding the fate of the store. It is my most sincere dying wish that Eden's be run by a new generation of women, and I hope that they will endeavor to make it as grand a success as it once was.'"

The words sank in and Jake could feel himself shrinking in his chair. The store had indeed gone to Sophie and Mindy. It had also gone to someone with whom he had zero relationship, someone he knew nothing about. Even worse, the heirs were required to keep the store running for another two years. There never was a deal for him to pursue. He'd never had a chance. And there was an excellent chance that this woman he'd fallen for, the one he couldn't get enough of, had known all along.

Ten

Sophie was frozen in shock. What had just happened? And what was she supposed to do about it? Her eyes glazed over. The room started to spin. Everything her grandmother had ever said to her echoed in her head. *You'll run Eden's one day, Sophie. You will.* She felt light-headed, as if she might faint. And then she heard a sound that yanked her back to her reality—her mother, sobbing.

"Mom. Mom. It's okay." Sophie reached out and rubbed her back. She had no reason to reassure her mom that anything would be okay, but it was her impulse to comfort her, if only to quiet her cries. It was adding an unbearable layer of awkward to the tension in the room.

Sophie's mom looked up at her with mascara

streaming down her face. Something about her pained expression made her look even more like Mindy, which was quite a feat. They were already near picture-perfect duplicates of each other. "I never wanted this to come out. But your grandmother never liked me. She never thought I was good enough for your father." Her mom whipped around and shot her own sister, Sophie's aunt Jill, the most glaring look. "You always had to have everything that was mine, didn't you?"

"Excuse me?" Jill answered with venom in her voice, pushing her chair back from the table and standing up straight. "You got everything from your husband. Everything. Meanwhile, I was paid off to lie to my own daughter about who her father was."

Ms. Adams, the lawyer who'd been leading the proceedings, stood and made her way over to Jill. "Ladies. I need to ask for civil discourse or I'm going to have to ask you to leave the premises."

Sophie couldn't believe what she was hearing. Her heart would have been a little more broken by each new revelation if her brain wasn't struggling so hard to put it all into context. Everything she thought she knew about her family was wrong. What other secrets were lurking between her mom and her aunt Jill? What else had her father done in his lifetime that would come back to haunt them all?

"You knew this was going to come out today, didn't you?" Mom asked Jill.

"Ladies…" Ms. Adams interjected with the leading tone required for a situation as tense as this.

"I had a pretty good idea, yes. And I have been waiting a very long time for it. Emma hasn't had the life she deserved. Now she'll have her birthright."

Her birthright. Anger began to bubble under Sophie's skin, a reaction that shocked her. She wasn't an angry person, but Eden's was also Sophie's birthright, something Sophie had dreamed about since she was a little girl. She'd put in the time over the last several years. She'd been the one at Gram's side, helping with the day-to-day, doing everything in her power to keep her grandmother's vision alive. It was one thing to have to share it with Mindy, the one who didn't care about it at all, the one who always had to be right and never gave Sophie the respect she deserved. It was another to have to share it with someone who might as well be a stranger.

Sophie scanned the conference table, and when she looked up, Emma was staring at her. Sophie's breath wasn't merely stuck in her chest. It felt as though it was never going to leave her body again. The look in Emma's eyes could only be described as disgust. Maybe even plain and simple hatred. Emma might have come here today in the hopes that a wrong would be righted, but Sophie was still getting up to speed. Much of the emotion coursing through Sophie had to do with confusion. She and Emma had never been close, partly because her mother and her sister had always kept their distance. If anything, their mother was more prone to disparaging comments uttered after one too many dirty martinis.

None of the bitterness between her mom and Aunt Jill made sense when Sophie was growing up. Now it was all coming together. Her mother had been living with the knowledge that her husband and her own sister had an affair. That made Sophie's mind run off on yet another tangent. How long did it go on? Was it a onetime thing? Or was their mother made to suffer that indignity on a regular basis while Mindy and Sophie were none the wiser?

Emma rose from her seat and looked down at her mother. "Let's go. We've gotten what we came for today." She then directed her sights at Sophie again. The fury in her eyes had faded, replaced by ice-cold determination. "Sophie. Mindy. I'll begin work at Eden's on the second of January. I expect to have an office. One that is no smaller or any less nice than either of yours. Please make the appropriate accommodations."

Sophie and Mindy exchanged glances. Sophie was surprised Mindy didn't lunge for her and tackle her right there in the conference room.

"Of course. That won't be a problem," Sophie replied, thinking that this was going to be nothing but a huge problem. Gram's office would have to become Emma's. That made Sophie's heart hurt. Still, she had to respect the wishes of the woman she loved and admired. If Gram wanted Emma to be part of the operation, there had to have been a reason for it. Gram must have believed that this could all work out. Sophie prayed that was true.

Sophie and Jake both got up from the table and

wandered out into the hall. She sought comfort in his arms the instant they were alone, but he stood straight as a board, putting only one arm around her, and even that wasn't a true embrace.

"I need a hug, Jake. I need reassurance right now. That was a complete nightmare."

He didn't say anything, but she felt the rise of his chest as he drew in a deep breath.

"Jake. Hug me. Say something. Please. Can't you see that I'm upset?" She took a half step back. He wouldn't even look her in the eye. "What is going on?"

Finally, their gazes connected. "What's the one thing you always told me when you talked about your grandmother?"

Sophie shrugged, unsure of why he would even ask this question. "I don't know. That I loved her more than anything?"

He nodded, slowly, but it wasn't so much agreement as it was confirmation that she was on the right track. "And?"

"That we were very close? That we talked all the time?"

"Exactly."

The air seemed to stand still as his one-word reply echoed in her head. "You think I knew about this business with my cousin being my half sister? Because I didn't. I am as shocked as anybody right now."

He rolled his eyes and turned away from her, running his hand through his hair. "Do you really expect me to believe that? What kind of family keeps that sort of thing a secret? All this time?"

"What kind of family? I don't know, Jake. Apparently mine. But don't act like this is somehow my fault. I knew nothing about it. Nothing."

A low grumble escaped Jake's lips. Suddenly that heavenly sound was no longer so pleasant. "Okay. Fine. I'll buy that much, but I am not about to buy the fact that you knew nothing about these stipulations about Eden's. You let me send you fruit baskets and bring you flowers and generally make a fool of myself when you knew that you were in no position to sell."

Sophie's eyebrows drew together. "I never asked you to do any of those things. If you acted foolishly, that was your doing, not mine. If you honestly think that I knew what was going to happen today, then I don't know what to say. If you think that little of me, we have a serious problem. A problem that goes well beyond flowers and fruit baskets."

"You talked about nothing but how close you and your grandmother were. It was the basis of your entire argument for not selling. I don't see any way you couldn't have known about this. All those years of working closely with her and she never said a thing to you about you having another sister? She never said anything about restricting the sale of the business when you inherited it? That seems like an awfully salient detail. I can't believe you didn't know about this. I don't see any way you didn't know."

Sophie wasn't sure she'd ever heard more hurtful words come out of Jake's mouth, aside from the morning after their first tryst eight years ago. "I can't believe you don't even care that I am deeply upset about what happened today."

"Why would you be upset? You got exactly what you wanted. Part ownership of a multibillion-dollar property, and two years to try to make it a success. You have an ironclad legal excuse to do exactly what you wanted all this time. You win, Sophie. You got everything you ever wanted today. The rest of us got screwed."

Hundreds of thoughts were colliding in Sophie's head. None of this made sense. The secrets. The will. Jake's anger. "You really think I got everything I ever wanted? Because that's not true." As her words left her mouth, the weight of what came next became unbearable. She would not get everything she wanted. Because what she truly wanted was Jake. And he thought she'd deceived him. He thought she was some sort of terrible conniving person when Sophie couldn't have been any less that if she tried.

"Just be honest about it, Soph. I can't stand the deception. You were never going to sell to me and you just let me believe there was still a chance."

That really got her blood boiling, even hotter than it had been when she started to think about Emma's claim on Sophie's birthright. "I told you from the beginning that I didn't want to sell. You just didn't want to listen. You knew that I was putty in your hands and you did everything you could to take advantage of that. If I'm guilty of letting you believe in anything, it's that I let you believe in us, Jake. And judging by this conversation, I guess I was wrong to do that."

"Why did you let me come here today, Sophie? To humiliate me? To make it that much worse when I call my business partners and tell them what an idiot I've been?" Jake's expression was unflinching. None of what Sophie was saying was making the slightest bit of an impression. That was the moment when she knew this was over.

"Do you honestly think I would do that? I'm not even capable of being that conniving." Sophie wrapped her arms around her waist. "You know what? You are just as much of a jerk now as you were eight years ago. You don't care about me. You don't care about my feelings or what I'm going through. I was just a foot in the door, wasn't I? A chance for you to make a big pile of money and be the big important man."

"Don't criticize me for being successful or good at what I do. That isn't what this conversation is about, okay? I need to know why you weren't honest with me. I need to know why you let me believe one thing when you knew all along that it was never going to happen."

An awkward and unexpected burst of laughter left Sophie's lips. She couldn't help it. The irony of this situation was not lost on her. In fact, it was slapping her in the face, and the sting was going to linger for a very long time. "Sort of what you did to me in school, isn't it? Be sweet to me and flirt all day long and let me be the girl who makes you feel good about yourself, but never actually give anything back."

"That's not the same thing at all."

Now the irony was eating away at Sophie's insides, hollowing her out. Jake was never going to take a leap with her. Even when this was so much better than last time, it wasn't what she really wanted it to be. It wasn't love, returned and given freely. It was love one way. She'd allowed her stupid optimism to get in the way of rational thought. Jake Wheeler wasn't capable of an emotional investment. Money, yes. His heart? No.

And to think she'd been prepared to profess her affection for him today. The universe's timing was impeccable. Here she was being pulled back from the precipice in the nick of time.

A smaller laugh left Sophie's lips. "It's funny, you know."

His vision narrowed on her. It was such a waste of his incredible eyes. "There's nothing funny about this."

Sophie threaded her arms into her coat, straightening her spine and forcing her tears back down her throat with nothing but sheer will. "Perhaps we'll find it funny later. Years from now. When it doesn't hurt so much."

"Sophie, you've lost me. And honestly, I don't have the patience for your clever games right now. If you want to tell me something, just say it and get it over with."

His voice sliced through the air like a sharpened

blade, destroying everything sweet and kind and beautiful between them. She was no longer sadly resigned to her fate. She was no longer going to be sweet, polite Sophie Eden. She'd had enough. "It's not a game, Jake. I was going to tell you today that I love you. But you have ruined that. For the second time in my life, actually. You have ripped it to hundreds of pieces. So instead, I'm going to say goodbye. Have a nice life. I never want to see you again."

She turned on her heel, the tears starting the instant she could afford to cry, when her face was turned away from Jake and she was marching down to the elevator.

"Sophie. Stop. Don't be so dramatic."

She couldn't turn back. She couldn't look at him. She couldn't see what she had so stupidly believed could be her future. Her life. It was just going to break her heart. She picked up her speed, turning the corner. The elevator door was closing. "Hold it, please!" she called out in desperation. A man stuck out his hand. With a lunge, Sophie's foot hit the inside of the car and she pulled the rest of herself through the narrow opening. She nearly collapsed against the back wall of the elevator. The doors closed.

"Are you okay, ma'am?"

Sophie straightened and smoothed down the front of her coat. She endeavored to keep her breaths even. She told herself that crying would have to be for later. Not now. She'd never be able to stop. "Oh, yes. I'm just fine. Thank you for holding the elevator." She turned and granted the man a small smile before opening her purse and rifling through it for a tissue.

The elevator dinged at the lobby floor. The man held the door for her. "No problem. Happy holidays."

"Happy holidays to you, too." For the first time ever, Sophie put no stock in the sentiments behind those words. As she strolled out into the biting-cold day, it felt as though the spirit of Christmas had not only been sucked out of her, it had been taken from the entire city. She not only couldn't conjure the feeling she looked forward to all year long, it was as if she couldn't even remember what it felt like. It was simply one more damning detail in her history with Jake. She loved him and he wasn't capable of giving it back. This time, recovering from the loss might take forever.

Jake took the stairs. He couldn't get in the elevator that Sophie had just ridden in. He already knew that his nose would betray him and pick up on any traces of her sweet scent. That would just bring back a flood of memories that did nothing to help him out of his predicament. It would do nothing to fix what had transpired over the last hour—the utter dismantling of the most vital plan he'd ever had.

Jake's driver was waiting for him at the curb outside the lawyer's office. Jake had hoped Sophie would be waiting as well, having remembered that they'd arrived together.

"Sir, I saw Ms. Eden come outside, but she didn't

say anything when I called out to her. She just kept going down the sidewalk."

"She had somewhere she had to be." Jake was quick with the excuse.

"I have never seen anyone walk so fast in heels. She was practically sprinting."

"It's in her DNA."

Just as fast and able in heels, Mindy stormed out of the building. The stretch SUV was back again. But Jake wanted a word with her before she got away.

"Mindy. Do you have a minute?"

She wrapped her arms around herself. "I have exactly that. I have to get back to my office."

"Did you know about all of this? Did you know all of that was going to happen?"

She shook her head so fast her hair went flying in the cold winter wind. "No, I didn't know. I was completely broadsided in there. And I'm furious with my sister. She had to have known that was going to happen. She was ridiculously close with our grandmother. I can't believe she never told me."

In any other situation, Jake would have felt vindicated by Mindy's statement. She was equally astounded by Sophie's deception. But he took no joy in the revelation. There was nothing good to get out of any of this. "I'm in shock. She definitely never gave me any indication that this would happen. Obviously, I never would have pursued the purchase if that were the case." Nor would he have pursued Sophie, which would have meant that his heart wouldn't be broken right now. "No wonder she was so willing to promise me she wouldn't cut a deal with any buyer without first talking to me. It meant nothing."

Mindy's eyes were wide as dinner plates. "She did what? She never told me that. How could she make that promise to you and not tell me?" Mindy looked over her shoulder at the car waiting for her. "I don't know what to tell you, Jake, other than today has been just as horrible for me as it has been for you. I'm going to have to sell my company or clone myself or something. I'm going to have to go to that store every day for the next two years and work with my sister, who I no longer trust, along with another sister I never even knew I had."

However upset he was with Sophie, Jake did realize that both she and Mindy had also taken a real beating today. "I'm sorry. I'm sorry for all of us."

Mindy returned her sights to him. "Yeah. Me, too. I sort of thought you two might figure out your issues this time. Looks like Sophie was the one to mess it up on this go-around, huh?"

Jake nodded, but he hated every word out of Mindy's mouth. It felt like she was sealing his fate. His deal was gone, and so was any chance at a future with Sophie. "I guess so." Out of the corner of his eye, he saw a door on the SUV open and out came a man he immediately recognized—Sam Blackwell. His blood began to boil. Sophie had told him that Mindy knew him only casually. Apparently that was not the case. "I think your ride is waiting for you."

Mindy glanced at the car and didn't turn back. "Oh, yes. I have to go. Take care of yourself." She trotted off and Sam stood aside and helped her into the car. Then it sped off.

Jake just stood there on the sidewalk, wondering how many more shocks he was going to have to withstand today. He couldn't take many more. Sophie had lied to him about Sam Blackwell, too.

"Mr. Wheeler? You ready?" David, his driver, called out.

"Yes." Jake got settled in the back seat of the car as David rounded to his door. He started to run over everything that had just happened, if only to try to make sense of it. The vision most easily conjured was one he hadn't actually seen—Sophie running down the street, away from him. It troubled him that his mind had no problem imagining her wanting to distance herself from him, forever. He looked out the window and ran his hand through his hair. What future did he have now? The business deal of a decade was officially dead. And any prospect of love was gone, as well.

"Back to the office, sir?"

"Yes, please." Jake had phone calls to make as soon as he returned. Phone calls that he dreaded making. No matter how hard he had tried in the past to shrug off failure, it always bothered him. None of his investment partners was going to listen to an excuse. They weren't going to listen to him explain how hard he had worked to put this deal together. He knew this because he knew this of himself. If the roles had been reversed, if he had been counting on someone else, he wouldn't want to hear excuses.

"How did things go at the lawyer's office?" Audrey asked when he returned.

"They could have gone better."

Audrey frowned and cocked her head to one side. "You missed Stephanie in Accounting's birthday. Would you like me to get you a piece of cake?"

"No, thank you. I'm not sure sugar is going to help me out now." All he could think about was that day at Eden House, making Christmas cookies. Talk about a slice of life he'd thought was never meant for him. But that was Sophie. She filled in the gaps, the things he'd missed out on. He hadn't needed sugar that day. He'd only needed her. And they had fit together so perfectly, it was hard to stomach the realization that she was gone from his life now.

"Coffee, then?" Audrey asked.

"Yes, actually. That would be great."

"Go ahead. I'll bring it in."

Jake stepped into his office and forced himself to move quickly, to sit behind his desk and pull out his phone and prepare to get this over with. These calls would not be pleasant, but there was very little of Jake's job that was fun. Today was a day for eating crow. Tomorrow he'd get up in the morning and do it all over again, hopefully with his pride intact.

The first few phone calls were irksome, but ultimately it all came down to business. He endured a few moments of disgruntlement, followed by the sentiment that everyone still wanted to keep working together. There was always money to be made.

They just had to find the next big deal. At least he had that much going for him.

More than one person expressed the hope that when the two years were up, Jake would still have the inside track. "Make sure you maintain that relationship," one of his fellow investors said. Jake wasn't about to get into it, but that relationship was gone. There would be no more Sophie in his life. Not after today.

He decided to reach out to Sawyer last. This call was going to be the most difficult, only because he admired Sawyer so much and they had become friends. "Hey, Jake. I was eagerly waiting for this phone call, but the truth is that I already heard through the grapevine about what happened with Victoria Eden's will."

Jake slumped back in his chair and raked his fingers through his hair. "News travels fast."

"Bad news travels fastest of all."

"So true."

"Are you holding up okay? I'm sure it's disappointing. You've put a lot of work into it."

"You know this game as well as anyone. Sometimes you work your tail off and it still doesn't work. This is just another of those instances." Except that it really wasn't. There was more to it. So much more. And he couldn't talk to anyone about it.

"Do you want to grab a beer after work? I'm over at the hotel. We could go up to the speakeasy and hole up in a corner booth."

Jake was always eager to get a drink with a colleague, especially someone he liked as much as Sawyer. But he hesitated, knowing that a beer or two might turn to truth serum in his veins, which might cause him to talk about things that weren't appropriate. The blowup with Sophie was still so fresh in his head, but it was as if it hadn't truly sunk in yet. If he tried hard enough, it might never do that.

"Jake? Everything okay?"

"Yeah. Sorry. I've got a lot on my mind right now."

Eleven

After the day Jake threw away their future, Sophie did the only thing she knew how to do. She threw herself into work. Unfortunately, work right now was like jumping into the deepest part of the ocean without a life vest. The days were long and brutally tiring. She spent more than one night on the couch in her office. She tried to ignore her memories of being with Jake on that couch, but then again, she was doing her level best to forget everything she ever knew about Jake Wheeler. He'd returned to the category of people to leave in the past. Forever. She simply couldn't be dumb enough to let him break her heart again. She couldn't afford to be so self-destructive.

She wasn't quite sure how she made it through the five days from December 18, the reading of Gram's will, to December 23, also known at Eden's as The Hardest Day of the Year. Customers were desperate to be done with their shopping, but their choices had dwindled considerably. Employees were exhausted after many long days spent on their feet dealing with short fuses and endless demands. Tomorrow, Christmas Eve, would be much better. Eden's was open for only a few hours, the crowds were always much smaller that day and most people were officially in the Christmas spirit.

Which was why December 23 was a day where Gram always went the extra mile. Complimentary fresh-baked cookies, hot cocoa and mulled cider were available on each floor of the store. That alone made such a huge difference—everything smelled heavenly. Santa no longer sat on his regal chair waiting for children to share their Christmas wishes. Instead, he roamed the store with a photographer elf, delivering candy canes and candid Polaroids, while spreading good cheer. Breakfast, lunch and dinner were brought in for the employees. Everyone earned time and a half.

Sophie's handling of December 23 was a test of whether she could match her grandmother's greatness. Could she keep everyone at Eden's, customers and employees alike, happy on the worst shopping day of the year? She only knew that she had to try, and even if she failed, it would keep her mind off the person she missed so desperately—Jake.

Arriving at the store that morning, running on a scant five hours of sleep and too much coffee, Sophie immediately noticed that something was off. Normally, salespeople and the department managers were buzzing about, busy as bees. Not now. Only a handful of employees were at their stations and the store was set to open in ten minutes. She made her way up to women's shoes and spotted Lizzie waiting for her, perched on one of the sofas. She popped up from her seat the instant she saw Sophie.

"I'm afraid I have bad news." Lizzie walked double time with Sophie back to the elevator.

"Do I even want to know?"

"Santa called in sick. It's impossible to find a replacement this close to Christmas. I tried."

Sophie blew out a breath and jabbed the button for the elevator. "Do we have anyone who can fill in?"

"I'm not sure."

"Reginald? Duane?"

Lizzie peered at Sophie as if she'd lost her mind. "Can you really see Reginald in the fur-trimmed suit? I think he'd rather die. As for Duane, he's too big for it."

"What about Theo in men's shoes?"

Lizzie nodded eagerly. "Good idea. I'll go talk to him after we discuss the bagel disaster."

"Disaster?"

"Mary's Bagels lost our order. They never showed up, and when I called, they said it was too late for them to deliver now. People are not happy. Everyone's waiting in the employee lounge, wondering where their food is."

"So that's why nobody's in their department. The

store opens in ten minutes. I'll call about the bagels. You tell everyone it's on the way."

"Got it."

Sophie and Lizzie stepped off the elevator and marched down the hall to Sophie's office. Sophie was already on the phone to Mary's.

"Mary's Bagels. This is Mary."

"Mary, hey. It's Sophie Eden. What happened?" Sophie tossed her purse onto her desk.

"When your grandmother passed away, one of my guys canceled your standing order. I don't know what to tell you."

"There's nothing you can do? I have a ton of hungry employees. I can't let this happen today." *Please not today.* Sophie had to at least show herself that she was capable of living up to what Gram would have done. This job and Eden's were the only things Sophie had right now, and somebody had to be competent going into next year. Mindy was bound to be difficult, and Emma was a wild card. "I will owe you, big-time, if you can make this happen."

Mary grumbled over the line. "I can get you four dozen now and the rest in an hour. It's the best I can do."

Gram never would have stood for this. There would have been hell to pay. But Sophie didn't have the energy to yell at anyone. "Thank you so much. And please, reinstate our order for next year." She hung up her phone and looked at Lizzie, who had just walked in. "Food is on the way. Hopefully that will be the worst of it. Can you please confirm lunch and dinner?"

"I'm on it." Lizzie turned on her heel and disappeared through the door.

Sophie plopped down in her chair. Through one of her office windows, she glimpsed snow flurries fluttering. This might end up being the prettiest, snowiest Christmas yet. Too bad she might have no Christmas to speak of at all. Her family was in tatters over everything that had come to light the day the will was read. Her mother wanted no part of celebrating. She was still too upset. Instead, she'd jetted off to Grand Cayman to spend the holiday drinking rum cocktails and lounging by the pool at a friend's villa. Mindy wasn't speaking to her at all. More than a dozen phone calls in five days had gone unreturned.

At this rate, Sophie would end up going to Eden House by herself. Sophie's preparations could very well be down the drain. Jake was wrong about a lot, but he might end up being right about one thing— decorating Eden House could very well have been a waste of time.

The mere thought of Jake made Sophie's stomach sour. It wasn't that Sophie had been looking forward to the holiday with him. He'd made it clear how much he disliked it and didn't care to participate. It was more that she'd looked forward to his being a part of her life this Christmas. There had been joy in knowing that she and her handsome Grinch had somehow miraculously found their way back to each other. Their future had been anything but sewn up, but there were glimmers of hope, and that was all she'd ever asked for.

But no. That wasn't the way things had played out. Although she would have far preferred to have learned about Emma while Gram was still alive, Sophie refused to blame the Jake situation on the will. He'd used it as an excuse to cut her out of his life. He'd been waiting for her to betray him, just so he could reaffirm his deep-seated belief that the people who mean the most ultimately let you down.

She and Jake simply weren't meant to be together, however much she wanted him and cared about him. It didn't matter that the last few weeks had been the best of her life. Whatever he was feeling, it clearly wasn't enough to make him want to stay in her life. It was just as true now as it had been years ago, but far more painful. She'd never find another love like Jake. The sooner she got used to it, the better.

Burying herself in the business of Eden's was the only thing that could save her now, so Sophie decided to walk the store, helping as needed. It was the sort of hands-on thing that Gram would have done in a pinch, and honestly it was a godsend. It kept Sophie so occupied that she worked right through lunch and well into the afternoon. She lent a hand at the gift wrapping station on the third floor, and helped customers at the perfume counter. She restocked gloves and scarves in ladies' accessories, and folded sweaters in the men's department. She forced a smile and soothed unruly customers by doling out discount shopping passes.

By four thirty, her stomach rumbled so loudly that a woman standing a good fifteen feet away from her must have heard it, because she shot her a look. She needed food.

She headed upstairs to the employee lounge, discovering that dinner had not yet been delivered and that lunch had largely been decimated. She grabbed a wheat roll and a pat of butter and scarfed it down. At least it would hold her over a bit longer.

She then trudged down the hall, so exhausted that she had to stop at Lizzie's desk and sit for a minute. "I don't know how my grandmother did it. I feel like I've been hit by a truck." Sophie kicked off her shoes, another of her favorite Blahniks, Mary Janes in turquoise suede with an adorable scalloped edge.

"I don't know how either of you managed a whole day in heels." Lizzie kicked her foot out from behind her desk to reveal a cute but sensible pair of black flats.

"Most days I don't even think about it." Sophie tapped her bare feet on the floor. "Lizzie, can I ask you a question?"

"Of course."

"You were at Eden's with my grandmother for five years before I worked here. You've seen a few of the ups and downs of the store. Do you think we can make it?"

Just then, Reginald breezed in from the elevator, wearing a kelly green suit that made him look like a towering, flamboyant elf. "Is it time to go home yet? I have had the worst day. A child climbed into one of the window displays and it took nearly an hour to convince him to come out."

Lizzie checked her phone. "Sorry. Another two hours until closing."

Reginald shook his head and took the seat next to Sophie. "What are we talking about? And please tell me we're gossiping about Barb and Mike in housewares. Those two? That's a love connection if ever I have seen one."

Sophie laughed. "Sorry. No gossip. In fact, I had to go and get serious on poor Lizzie."

"We were discussing whether or not Eden's can make it," Lizzie said.

Reginald crossed his legs and looked over at Sophie, past his glasses perched on the edge of his nose. "This business is a roller coaster. That is nothing new. The sooner you get used to it, the better."

Sophie nodded slowly, not sure if that made her feel any better at all. "I know. You're right."

"But let me tell you this. First off, I have a lot of friends who do what I do. People don't know it, but the world of window dressing is incredibly tight-knit." He gently rested his hand on Sophie's forearm. "None of my friends works in a store as special as Eden's. Your grandmother knew what she was doing. Her spirit is in every square inch of this place."

Sophie had to wonder if Reginald had any idea how unencouraging his pep talk was. This all seemed like more confirmation that Sophie would never live up to the specter of her grandmother.

"But I can also tell you that I've seen a big change

in this store over the last three years. A big change. Lizzie, I'm sure you noticed it, too."

Lizzie nodded and looked at Sophie, seeming resigned. "I have."

Sophie's heart felt heavy. Would she ever be able to overcome the challenges facing the store? Especially now that she was going to have to work with Mindy, who would be digging in her heels the whole way? And what about Emma? Sophie hardly knew her. Now they were supposed to save the family business together? "I know. It's the downturn in retail. I don't know how we're going to get through it. It's not just the store. It's a market condition. I suppose we just have to ride it out."

Reginald pursed his lips. "Please. Downturn in retail. There have been a million of those. In the end, people will always love to shop. It's the hunter-gatherer in all of us. I wasn't talking about that. I was talking about you."

"Me?"

He nodded, and for an instant Sophie thought she saw his eyes mist up. "Your grandmother was a new woman when you came to work here. She was energized. It was like she was twenty years younger."

"I never noticed any difference in her," Sophie said.

"That's because you weren't here to see her at work in the years before that. She believed in you. She believed that there was a future for this store when you came to work here. You had ideas. You had enthusiasm. She loved every second of it."

Sophie remembered so clearly the day her grandmother finally asked her to come to work for the store. It had always been the plan for Sophie to start right after business school, but it hadn't played out that way. Gram had other employees in the role that Sophie would eventually play, so she had to wait until they moved on. Sophie spent three years aimlessly shuffling from corporate job to corporate job, waiting for her chance. When she got it, she leaped at it.

Unfortunately, having a job she'd been predestined for had made Sophie discount the times when her grandmother said she was lucky to have Sophie there. She'd assumed that was her grandmother speaking, not her boss. Now she knew that Gram had meant it.

"Why do you think she didn't tell me? About Emma or the stipulation about keeping the store open for two years?"

"My guess is she thought she had time. Everybody thinks they have time. And honestly, she had no reason to believe otherwise. She was so full of life. That's part of what made it such a shock."

Sophie nodded. She would have cried if she had the energy. She'd shed everything she had for Jake over the past few days. Still, it all made perfect sense. Gram would have eventually told her. But she thought she had time. Just then, Sophie's cell phone rang. She fished it out of the pocket of her dress. *Look who finally decided to call me back.* "I need to take this. It's my sister."

"Which one?" Reginald quipped.

Sophie started back to her office. "Funny. That's funny." She answered the call and shut her office door behind her. "Did you lose your phone? Or were you merely torturing me?"

"I needed time to think."

Skipping her desk, Sophie stretched out on her couch and put her feet up. "You could have called me and told me that, you know."

"I was angry. I didn't want to say something ugly."

"Gram's will is not my fault."

"I know that. But I was pretty sure you'd hidden those stipulations from me. You and Gram talked about everything."

Sophie kneaded her forehead. "Not everything."

"Really, Soph? Because I really want to believe you, but I still need to hear it from you."

"I did not know about any of it. I'll take a lie detector test if you want me to. I swear I didn't know."

Mindy blew out a breath. "Okay. I believe you. Thank you."

"I'm glad that's cleared up." It was then that Sophie realized just how much it might not have been ridiculous for Jake to arrive at the same conclusion as Mindy. Sophie and her sister had known each other for their entire lives, and Mindy still thought Sophie had pulled the wool over everyone's eyes. "Are you still coming up to Eden House tomorrow?"

Mindy sighed. "I'm not. I need a break from family, and I made plans to spend it with a friend."

Sophie's heart sank to her stomach. "What am I supposed to do with your gifts?"

"Give them to me for my birthday? I haven't even had time to shop for you, so I don't have the same problem. I'm sorry. I think we just need to pretend like Christmas doesn't even exist this year."

Christmas doesn't exist. Sophie couldn't have thought up a more depressing concept if she tried. "Fine. I'll celebrate by myself."

"What about Jake? Did you not patch things up?"

"No, we didn't patch things up. You would have known that if you'd called me back. We're done."

"Oh. Wow. I'm sorry. I just assumed you guys would get back together. You seemed so...happy."

A headache the size of the women's shoe department was now brewing in Sophie's head. "Funny, but he's holding the same grudge you were. Maybe you two should spend some time together."

"I'm so sorry. I, uh, well, I might not have made plans if I'd known. Please don't be mad."

"Don't be mad? I feel like I'm the only one trying to hold everything together. Our family. The store." Sophie could feel herself unraveling. Between her lack of sleep and everything that had gone wrong, she wasn't far from coming apart at the seams.

"I'll make it up to you next year. I'm sorry, but that's my decision. And I have to go. I'm meeting my friend. I'm going to be late."

Sophie didn't have the strength to argue. "Fine. Merry Christmas." It wasn't like her at all, but she hung up on Mindy and dropped her phone on the floor.

She rolled to her side and held her hand to her

chest, her breaths coming out of her in fits. From across the room, the lights on her office Christmas tree were twinkling like everything in the world was okay. But it wasn't. The tears were coming now, and she couldn't do anything to stop them. Everything that was *wrong* in her life and *gone* from her life was too much. Gram. Jake. Now Christmas.

Twelve

Jake was typically alone in his office on Christmas Eve, and this year was no different. His employees were either traveling or already at home with their families. Jake used the day to catch up on projects he'd put off. He took some time to finish up his projections for the new year. Basically, anything that could keep his mind off Christmas.

He'd told himself that he wouldn't work a full day, but now that it was noon, he didn't really see any reason to go home. What was waiting for him there? Nothing. No Sophie, that was for sure. But he did need lunch, and for that he'd need to run down the block to the deli.

Outside, it was bitter cold. Yesterday's snow had been mostly swept from the sidewalks, but it remained along the curbs, piled up and waiting to melt. Across the street in the park, the holiday market was bustling as always, but it would be closed in an hour or two. Another reminder of this season he had to withstand every year would be gone. It would be worse next year because now Christmas would just remind him of Sophie. She had not only put her mark on him, but she would forever be inextricably linked to December 25.

He grabbed a turkey sandwich and was trekking back to the office when his phone rang. He had to wrestle his glove from his hand in order to dig his cell out of his pocket and answer.

"Hello?" His breath was a puff of white in the cold air as he continued to walk.

"Jake. It's Mindy Eden."

He came to a stop in the middle of the sidewalk. This was not a call he'd expected. "Mindy. Hi."

"Do you have a minute?"

Jake nearly laughed. Today, he had nothing but time. "Of course."

"Good. Because I talked to Sophie yesterday and I can't stop thinking about you two."

"What about us? Your sister and I are no longer involved."

"I know. And that's the problem."

"She told me she never wanted to see me again. I don't really know how I'm supposed to come back from that. She ran away in heels down a snowy New York street to prove her point."

"Sophie runs in heels all the time. That should

not be the measure of whether or not she actually meant what she said."

The cold was getting to Jake, so he put his glove back on and resumed the walk back to his office. "I wasn't very kind to her that day, either. I accused her of lying, and I wish I could take it back. I was upset and I said some stupid things."

"Do you still think she lied?"

Jake strolled back into his building and wandered off to the side of the lobby. "Honestly? I don't believe that your sister has an insincere or dishonest bone in her body. I don't know what the hell I was thinking."

"I'm glad to know it's not just me who's feeling like a jerk for not believing her. I apologized yesterday, though. I'm wondering if you shouldn't do the same."

He shook his head. "Do you think she would actually listen to me?"

"Sounds to me like you're asking whether or not she'll take you back. That I can't answer. But I do think she would at least let you apologize, which could be just what she needs. It might make her Christmas less miserable."

Jake laughed. A miserable Christmas? For Sophie? That seemed as unlikely a scenario as a repeat of yesterday's snowstorm in July.

"I'm serious, Jake. She's going to be all alone unless she can convince Barry to come and hang out with her. She's going to Eden House by herself."

"Where are you going to be? What about your mom?"

Mindy explained that her mom had taken off for the Caribbean and Mindy was opting for Miami with a friend. In fact, they'd both already left the city. Neither of them was feeling either the Christmas spirit or the joy of being a member of the Eden family.

This was not adding up for Jake. The Edens were solid as a rock, or so he had thought. Sophie had painted visions of a Christmas filled with love and laughter, of a house where everyone was happy and safe. And she wouldn't have that this year. Her Christmas was going to be just as terrible as Jake's, except it meant so much more to her.

"Where's Sophie now? Has she left for Eden House already?"

"I think the store is open until two today. Knowing her, she'll stay until closing and then she'll leave."

Jake was certain of very little right now, but the mere thought of Sophie suffering and being unhappy made his chest ache, and that could mean only one thing. He wasn't merely falling for Sophie. He loved her. And the only way to prove it was to save the thing he'd once despised. He was going to have to save Christmas.

"Mindy. I have to go. I hope you have fun in Miami with Sam Blackwell. Just be careful. He's not my favorite person. You can tell him I said that, too."

"How do you know I'm with Sam?"

"I pay attention. That's how." Jake marched over to the security desk. "We'll have to talk about this later. If I'm going to catch your sister at the store, I need to go now."

"Thanks, Jake."

"For what?"

"For being a good enough guy to want to make my sister happy."

He laughed again, much more readily this time. If he was being honest, he'd always been that guy. He'd always wanted to make Sophie happy. He'd just been doing an exceptionally poor job of it. "No problem." Jake hung up the phone and offered his deli bag to the female security guard working today. "Turkey on rye? Kosher dill on the side?"

She eyed him with suspicion. "What's the catch?"

"No catch. Just spreading a little holiday cheer." He was surprised to learn it didn't sound nearly as corny as he'd feared.

The guard dropped her steely stare and she smiled. "Thank you so much. I hope you have a merry Christmas."

"Thanks. I'm hoping so, too."

With no time to waste, Jake rushed back outside and down Fifth Avenue to Fortieth Street and the south side of the park. He was nearly to the Sixth Avenue corner when he spied the shop where Sophie had bought her ornament. The star. There was no telling if Barry had ever tracked down Sophie's grandmother's tree topper. Even if Sophie might not accept his apology, she might accept one final gift from him. It couldn't be met with any worse a reaction than a fruit basket.

He sprinted to the corner and back along the walkway, squeezing past people doing their last-minute shopping. When he got to the kiosk, a man was locking up the door.

"Please don't close the store. I need something," Jake blurted.

The man rolled his eyes. "We're basically sold out of everything. Sorry. Come see us next year."

Jake stepped right in front of him and looked him square in the eye. "You don't understand. I have to save Christmas for a very special woman. And if I don't, well, I might end up living my entire life alone."

"I'm sure that whatever you want is gone."

Jake could see it through the window. "It's not gone. It's right there. The gold star on top of that tree."

"We don't sell those. It's just for display."

"I'll give you a hundred bucks for it."

"Sir…"

"Two hundred. Cash."

"I wouldn't even know how to ring it up."

"Three hundred. I don't need a receipt. Trust me, I'm not going to bring it back."

The man closed his eyes and shook his head, just long enough to make Jake sick to his stomach. "All right. Fine." He turned the key and opened the door. "I'll be right back."

Jake watched as the man got out a stepladder, climbed to the top and removed the star from the top of the tree. He returned with Jake's purchase.

"Do you have a bag or a gift box?"

"No. Sorry."

Jake fished the cash out of his wallet and handed it over. "No worries. Thanks for your help."

With the gold star tucked under his arm, he broke free of the holiday market crowd and started to jog down Fortieth. When he got to the corner of Seventh Avenue, he spotted people with arms loaded down with Eden's shopping bags. The store was only three blocks down the avenue. Jake hurried to get there, his breath coming out in lofty puffs of white while the brisk wind whipped at his cheeks. The massive stone structure with the signature black-and-white Eden's sign hanging from the corner of the building loomed larger. It looked exactly as it had weeks ago, except Jake realized that he no longer saw it the same way. It was no longer a deal to be had. This was Sophie's whole life. He had to wonder if she would make room in that life for him or if he'd used up all of his chances. She'd told him a week ago that she intended to tell him that she loved him. Did she still feel that way? Or had he ruined everything?

He tried to imagine that day from Sophie's side of things. If it had gone as Jake had presumed it would, that would have been a difficult day for her. Mindy had given her ultimatum, which meant Sophie would have been scrambling for $2 billion. Granted, Jake could have bought Mindy out, but that wasn't a solution, either. That wasn't what Sophie wanted. It wasn't what her grandmother had envisioned. She'd wanted the granddaughters to run the store together. As a team. Now that team had one more person, someone she didn't know or trust. He'd been much too hard on Sophie. He knew that now.

He was steps from the revolving door when he came to a stop. He hadn't looked at the window displays the other times he'd been to the store. Not once. But here were crowds of people admiring them, pointing, taking pictures and raving. Children rushed from one window to another. They jumped up and down. There was so much joy and happiness around him. You could feel it in the air. For a moment, he allowed himself to simply soak it up. To drink it in. He'd been missing out on this because he'd decided as a young boy that it wasn't meant for him. Money and prestige were the things he'd been dead set on acquiring, just to prove to himself that he was stronger than his lot in life. In the meantime, he'd forgotten the part about being happy.

But it had found him with Sophie. She was his ray of sunshine. She was the reason that those two years of business school had been some of the best in his entire life. She made him look forward to things, even if it was merely looking forward to the chance to see her. He couldn't postpone happiness anymore. He had to grab it now.

He burst through the revolving doors and ran back to the elevators that went up to the offices. When he reached the top floor, there was nobody there. It was eerily quiet. For a split second, he thought he was too late. But then he turned and saw the light filtering from her office. Taking long strides, he arrived at her door, but she wasn't at her desk. She was asleep on her couch.

He crept into the room and set the star on her desk, taking a second to admire how beautiful she was when she was peacefully sleeping. He couldn't believe the way his heart swelled in his chest just to see her. So this really was love. He'd done more than fall for her. He was head-to-toe in love.

Not wanting to scare her, he cleared his throat. She stirred, but then snuggled up with the pillow again. The second time, he coughed. That was enough to make her open one eye.

"Jake." Sophie sat up, blinking, adorably sleepy. Her vision narrowed on him. "Why are you here?"

It wasn't exactly the greeting he'd hoped for, but honestly, it just felt good to be near her. He sat on the edge of the sofa near her feet and looked into her beautiful eyes. "I'm here because I'm a jerk."

"You are?" She sat up straighter, waking up. "Actually, you're right. You are a jerk."

Again, not what he'd wanted to hear, but better to face the music than lose out on a second, or technically a third, chance with Sophie. "I never should have doubted that you were just as surprised as I was by what was in your grandmother's will. But more important than that, I never, ever should have put a deal before my friendship with you. I never should have let it matter when I had a chance at more with you."

"Then why did you do it?"

Still unsure how she was feeling, he fought his

deep longing to take her hand. He needed her to understand how much he meant what he was about to say, but he'd have to let her decide on his sincerity for herself. "I did it because that was the part I knew I could make work. Give me numbers and a business or a piece of property and I will turn it into more. It was us that I didn't know how to turn into more. And frankly, I was terrified of more. I was scared of hurting you, or you hurting me, or something coming along and ruining everything. I played it safe, Sophie, and you know that's not me."

"I'm so happy to hear that you've figured it out. Really. I am. I'm happy for you."

"I was hoping you'd be happy for us." Jake looked into her warm eyes, hoping and praying that there was forgiveness in what she'd said. He wanted his third chance. More than anything. "Say something."

"It's kind of amazing that after all of that, I still missed you."

"You did?"

She gently swatted him on the arm and moved closer, her sweet scent making the moment that much more powerful. He wanted this more than anything.

"Of course I did. I missed you all those years we were apart. I missed you when I'd only known you for a day. That's what you do to me, Jake. You make me miss you, even when you're a jerk."

"Does that mean you'll give me a third chance?"

"That depends. Are you going to be needing a fourth one? Because if you are, I might have to pass. I can't do this again. It will kill me."

"I don't need a fourth chance. I promise." He bundled her in his arms and kissed her deeply. It was more than passion or heat; it was his chance to tell her without words that she was his world. "I love you, Sophie. I nearly said it weeks ago and I really wish I had."

"You do?" Tears welled in her eyes. He tried to kiss them away.

"I do."

"Thank God. I love you, too. And it has not been easy to convince myself otherwise. I have failed completely."

He smiled. "That's one thing I'd like to see you fail at."

Sophie glanced over at her desk and her brow furrowed. "What's that?"

Jake hopped up from the couch. "I brought you a gift."

"I told you that you didn't need to bring me presents every time you come to my office."

He picked up the tree topper and handed it to her. Her mouth went slack with surprise. "Oh, my God. The star from the market. You got it for me?"

"It's insurance. I didn't want to risk you not having a good Christmas, and I knew that having a star on the tree was important to you."

"That was so sweet of you, but you know, Christmas is already pretty much ruined. My mom and Mindy aren't coming."

"I know. I spoke to Mindy today."

"You did? Is that what finally made you get off your butt and get over here?"

Jake laughed. "Something like that." He put his arm around her and kissed her forehead. "And you know, we can save Christmas. Together."

"But you hate it."

He shook his head. "I am determined to change my thinking. But I'm going to need a few days at Eden House with you if I'm going to do it right."

Sophie's expression was one of happiness, delight and sheer thankfulness. "You'll come with me? You'll save Christmas?"

"As unlikely as that sounds, I don't want anything else."

Thirteen

The sky was pitch-black by the time Sophie and Jake made the trip down the driveway at Eden House. This was not how Sophie had envisioned arriving this year, in the car with Jake, looking forward to several days of just the two of them, alone. This holiday was going to be very different. There was no denying that. Nor was there any denying that it was a good thing. Everything else in her life was changing—why not Christmas, too?

"Good to be back?" Jake asked as he pulled under the porte cochere and parked the car.

She took a moment to look at him, still in awe that several hours ago she was out cold in her office, having lulled herself to sleep by trying to wish away the holiday she loved so much. Thank goodness Jake not only recognized the error of his ways, he had the nerve to show up at her office and apologize, just in the nick of time. There really were Christmas miracles.

"It's absolutely fantastic to be back."

Jake brought in their suitcases and took them up to Sophie's room while she unloaded the groceries they'd bought at the market in town for their Christmas Day feast. Luckily, they'd grabbed dinner during their drive up, so she wouldn't have to cook tonight. For tomorrow, she planned to prepare the same elegant meal Gram always made—beef tenderloin roasted with carrots and fresh herbs, along with a homemade potato gratin and sautéed green beans. For dessert, she needed only to reach into the freezer.

"Ooh. I forgot there were cookies." Jake wrapped his arms around her from behind as she placed the tin on the counter to thaw.

"Now you're happy I made you bake with me."

"I am." He kissed her neck. "I'm also wondering when we get to go upstairs and make up for real."

Sophie turned in his arms, fighting a smile. That smoldering look in his eyes was going to kill her. "There's a protocol to the Eden family Christmas, and that will have to wait just a little bit longer."

"Well, that might need to change if I have anything to say about it."

"I promise you the to-do list is much shorter now than it was the last time you were here."

Jake cast his sights up to the ceiling. "Thank God. So what do I need to do?"

"Nothing too arduous. It's tradition that we build a fire in the sitting room, drink champagne and talk about what we're thankful for."

"That's it?"

Sophie nodded. "Hardly any trouble at all. It'll mean a lot to me, though. It's exactly what we would be doing if Gram was here."

"I'm on fire duty." Jake disappeared into the utility room.

Sophie pulled out a bottle of Krug and placed it on the silver serving tray along with two champagne flutes. She also took a handful of cookies from the tin and put them on a plate. Once the fire got going, she figured they'd no longer be frozen. By the time she reached the sitting room, Jake was already hard at work placing the logs and crumpling newspaper. Sophie sat and opened the champagne as the fire started to crackle and pop.

"It'll be going in no time," he said, joining her on the couch.

"You seem remarkably happy." She poured them each a glass of champagne.

He picked up his glass but didn't drink from it yet. He simply looked at her, scanning her face, breaking her down with his eyes. "I am happy. I think this is the one time in my life I've ever felt hopeful. Truly hopeful. I can't explain it. I guess it's just being in love." He leaned forward and kissed her softly on the lips. "Which really just means that it all comes down to you. You make me feel hopeful."

Sophie smiled and kissed him again before raising

her glass. "To feeling hopeful." With a soft musical clink, they toasted, then each took a sip.

Jake predictably went for a cookie soon after. "These really are good. Is there some reason you can't have them year-round? I mean, are they just for Christmas?"

Sophie laughed. "If you like them that much, I will make them more often. Valentine's Day. Easter. Whatever you want."

"Thanksgiving. Arbor Day. There are a lot of holidays we could exploit in the interest of cookies."

She sat back on the couch and watched him as he happily polished off his treat. She loved seeing him like this—relaxed, fun Jake was the absolute best. "Do you feel like you already said what you're thankful for? Or is there more?"

He cast a look at her that was one-half genuine warmth and one-half seduction. It sent zaps of electricity down her legs. "I have a feeling there will always be more to be thankful for if I'm with you." He scooted closer to her on the couch. "What about you?"

Sophie sighed. This year had been crazy. A roller coaster unlike anything she'd ever experienced. Losing Gram, gaining a half sister, inheriting Eden's and having Jake return to her life. It was hard to believe she'd not only crammed it into twelve months, but this had been only the last three. And there was no sign of things slowing down anytime soon. Luckily, she'd have Jake by her side.

"I'm thankful for love. I'm thankful that I had

my family's love and I'm thankful that I now have yours. That's the greatest gift of all. It's all I've ever wanted."

He put his arm around her and pulled her close. "That's so perfect."

"Yeah? It was pretty simple, but that's all it boils down to."

He nodded and looked off at the fire. "How are you feeling about the challenges ahead? Your sister. Emma. Eden's. It's a lot to think about."

She could only nod in agreement. "It is. I'd be lying if I said that I wasn't worried at least a little bit. The unknown is scary. I don't want to spend the next two years waging battle with Mindy. And Emma? There's no telling what that's going to be like. She sure didn't seem warm and fuzzy at the lawyer's office that day."

"Well, as someone with their fair share of family upheaval, and a dad who wasn't in their life, I'm guessing there are probably some pretty big scars there. I'd try to give her the benefit of the doubt if you can."

Sophie didn't want to think about it too hard. She would just have to cling to optimism and hope that would get her through. "I can do that. For a little while, at least."

"Whatever happens, I want you to know I'll be with you every step of the way."

"What about two years from now? The building and the land will still be there, except then it will be ripe for the picking."

"I want what you want, Sophie. I am fully prepared to help you with the store in any way I can if that's what you want."

"It is what I want. More than almost anything. I mean, I don't want that more than I want you."

"I don't want anything more than you. And as for two years from now, I'm hoping we'll be in this exact spot talking about our future again, except maybe we'll be married by then and talking about kids."

Sophie was flat-out shocked. "That's quite the leap for you, Jake."

"It is. But I don't want to put off happiness anymore. We've both waited plenty long."

"A family? On top of the crazy lives we already have?"

"Don't you want this house to be full of love and laughter again? Like it was when you were a kid?"

"I do. Although one could argue that it's already full of love."

"That is the sweetest thing you could ever say. Now I just need to make you laugh." He tickled her on her sides and Sophie erupted into laughter, folding in half and trying to get away from his hands. She jerked, falling back onto the couch. Jake climbed on top of her and slid his hand under her sweater, still tickling, although it was quickly turning into more. He planted a hot kiss on her mouth, encouraging her lips apart with his tongue. She wanted him so badly she could hardly see straight. But there was one more thing that had to be done.

"Jake. We need to put the star on the tree before we can go up to bed."

"Who says we have to go up to bed? This couch is working great for me right now. We have all night, after all." He nuzzled her neck with his nose, driving her wild.

"I'm serious. Just this one thing. Then I promise you that clothes can come off."

She had never seen a human being hop off a piece of furniture so fast in her life. "The star on the tree and that's it?"

"Scout's honor." Sophie got up from the couch and took the star from the top of the bar, where Jake had left it. "I should probably get the stepladder. Unless you think you can reach it."

"First off, you should be the one to put the star on the tree. And second, I do not want to wait for one of us to get a stepladder. Come here." Jake wrapped his arms around her legs and hoisted her up.

It felt momentous to do this with him, with the star he had bought for her. It felt like a new beginning. "I love it. It's perfect. It might even be better than the old one. Gram would have approved."

"Good." He gently set her back down on her feet but kept her in his arms. "Have I told you how happy I am to be here with you? To have you share this with me? It means the world. Truly."

"Does this mean you might start liking Christmas?"

"Are you kidding? With you, Christmas is going to become my favorite day of the year."

"You're saying that so I'll go upstairs with you." She rose up onto her tiptoes and gave him a kiss that said that upstairs was the only place she wanted to go.

"Whatever it takes, Sophie. Whatever it takes."

* * * * *

In her brand-new series, New York Times
*bestselling author Brenda Jackson welcomes you
to Catalina Cove, where even the biggest
heartbreaks can be healed...*

Turn the page for a sneak peek at
Love in Catalina Cove

CHAPTER ONE

New York City

VASHTI ALCINDOR SHOULD be celebrating. After all, the official letter she'd just read declared her divorce final, which meant her three-year marriage to Scott Zimmons was over. Definitely done with. As far as she was concerned the marriage had lasted two years too long. She wouldn't count that first year since she'd been too in love to dwell on Scott's imperfections. Truth be told there were many that she'd deliberately overlooked. She'd been so determined to have that happily-ever-after that she honestly believed she could put up with anything.

But reality soon crept into the world of make-believe, and she discovered she truly couldn't. Her husband was a compulsive liar who could look you right in the eyes and lie with a straight face. She didn't want to count the number of times she'd caught him in the act. When she couldn't take the deceptions any longer she had packed her things and left. When her aunt Shelby died five months later, Scott felt entitled to half of the inheritance Vashti received in the will.

It was then that Vashti had hired one of the best divorce attorneys in New York, and within six weeks his private investigator had uncovered Scott's scandalous activities. Namely, his past and present affair with his boss's wife. Vashti hadn't wasted any time making Scott aware that she was not only privy to this information, but had photographs and videos to prove it.

Knowing she wouldn't hesitate to expose him as the lowlife that he was, Scott had agreed to an uncontested divorce and walked away with nothing. The letter she'd just read was documented proof that he would do just about anything to hold on to his cushy Wall Street job.

Her cell phone ringing snagged her attention, the ringtone belonging to her childhood friend and present Realtor, Bryce Witherspoon. Vashti clicked on her phone as she sat down at her kitchen table with her evening cup of tea. "Hey, girl, I hope you're calling with good news."

Bryce chuckled. "I am. Someone from the Barnes Group from California was here today and—"

"California?"

"Yes. They're a group of developers that's been trying to acquire land in the cove for years. They made you an unbelievably fantastic offer for Shelby by the Sea."

Vashti let out a loud shout of joy. She couldn't believe she'd been lucky enough to get rid of both her
ex-husband and her aunt's property in the same day.

"Don't get excited yet. We might have problems,"
Bryce said.

Vashti frowned. "What kind of problems?"

"The developers want to tear down your aunt's
bed-and-breakfast and—"

"Tear it down?" Vashti felt a soft kick in her
stomach. Selling her aunt's bed-and-breakfast was
one thing, having it demolished was another. "Why
would they want to tear it down?"

"They aren't interested in the building, Vash.
They want the eighty-five acres it sits on. Who
wouldn't with the Gulf of Mexico in its backyard? I
told you it would be a quick sale."

Vashti had known someone would find Shelby by
the Sea a lucrative investment but she'd hoped somehow the inn would survive. With repairs it could be
good as new. "What do they want to build there instead?"

"A luxury tennis resort."

Vashti nodded. "How much are they offering?"
she asked, taking a sip of her tea.

"Ten million."

Vashti nearly choked. "Ten million dollars? That's
nearly double what I was asking for."

"Yes, but the developers are eyeing the land next
to it, as well. I think they're hoping that one day
Reid Lacroix will cave and sell his property. When
he does, the developers will pounce on the opportu-

nity to get their hands on it and build that golf resort they've been trying to put there for years. Getting your land will put their foot in the door so to speak."

Vashti took another sip of her tea. "What other problems are there?"

"This one is big. Mayor Proctor got wind of their offer and figured you might sell. He's calling a meeting."

"A meeting?"

"Yes, of the Catalina Cove zoning board. Although they can't stop you from selling the inn, they plan to block the buyer from bringing a tennis resort in here. The city ordinance calls for the zoning board to approve all new construction. This won't be the first time developers wanted to come into the cove and build something the city planners reject. Remember years ago when that developer wanted to buy land on the east end to build that huge shopping mall? The zoning board stopped it. They're determined that nothing in Catalina Cove changes."

"Well, it should change." As far as Vashti was concerned it was time for Mayor Proctor to get voted out. He had been mayor for over thirty years. When Vashti had left Catalina Cove for college fourteen years ago, developers had been trying to buy up the land for a number of progressive projects. The people of Catalina Cove were the least open-minded group she knew.

Vashti loved living in New York City where things were constantly changing and people embraced those changes. At eighteen she had arrived in the city to attend New York University and remained after getting a job with a major hotel chain. She had worked her way up to her six-figure salary as a hotel executive. At thirty-two she considered it her dream job. That wasn't bad for someone who started out working the concierge desk.

"Unless the Barnes Group can build whatever they want without any restrictions, there won't be a deal for us."

Vashti didn't like the sound of that. Ten million was ten million no matter how you looked at it. "Although I wouldn't want them to tear down Shelby, I think my aunt would understand my decision to do what's best for me." And the way Vashti saw it, ten million dollars was definitely what would be best for her.

"Do you really think she would want you to tear down the inn? She loved that place."

Vashti knew more than anyone how much Shelby by the Sea had meant to her aunt. It had become her life. "Aunt Shelby knew there was no way I would ever move back to Catalina Cove after what happened. Mom and Dad even moved away. There's no connection for me to Catalina Cove."

"Hey, wait a minute, Vash. I'm still here."

Vashti smiled, remembering how her childhood friend had stuck with her through thick and thin. "Yes, you're still there, which makes me think you need your head examined for not moving away when you could have."

"I love Catalina Cove. It's my home and need I remind you that for eighteen years it was yours, too."

"Don't remind me."

"Look, I know why you feel that way, Vash, but are you going to let that one incident make you have ill feelings about the town forever?"

"It was more than an incident, Bryce, and you know it." For Vashti, having a baby out of wedlock at sixteen had been a lot more than an incident. For her it had been a life changer. She had discovered who her real friends were during that time. Even now she would occasionally wonder how different things might have been had her child lived instead of died at birth.

"Sorry, bad choice of words," Bryce said, with regret in her voice.

"No worries. That was sixteen years ago." No need to tell Bryce that on occasion she allowed her mind to wander to that period of her life and often grieved for the child she'd lost. She had wanted children and Scott had promised they would start a family one day. That had been another lie.

"Tell me what I need to do to beat the rezoning board on this, Bryce," Vashti said, her mind made up.

"Unfortunately, to have any substantial input, you need to meet with the board in person. I think it will be beneficial if the developers make an appearance, as well. According to their representative, they're willing to throw in a few perks that the cove might find advantageous."

"What kind of perks?"

"Free membership to the resort's clubhouse for the first year, as well as free tennis lessons for the kids for a limited time. It will also bring a new employer to town, which means new jobs. Maybe if they were to get support from the townsfolk, the board would be more willing to listen."

"What do you think are our chances?"

"To be honest, even with all that, it's a long shot. Reid Lacroix is on the board and he still detests change. He's still the wealthiest person in town, too, and has a lot of clout."

"Then why waste my and the potential buyer's time?"

"There's a slim chance time won't be wasted. K-Gee is on the zoning board and he always liked you in school. He's one of the few progressive members on the board and the youngest. Maybe he'll help sway the others."

Vashti smiled. Yes, K-Gee had liked her but he'd liked Bryce even more and they both knew it. His real name was Kaegan Chambray. He was part of the Pointe-au-Chien Native American tribe and his family's ties to the cove and surrounding bayou went back generations, before the first American settlers.

Although K-Gee was two years older than Vashti and Bryce, they'd hung together while growing up. When Vashti had returned to town after losing her baby, K-Gee would walk Vashti and Bryce home from school every day. Even though Bryce never said, Vashti suspected something happened between

Bryce and K-Gee during the time Vashti was away at that unwed home in Arkansas.

"When did K-Gee move back to Catalina Cove, Bryce?"

"Almost two years ago to help out his mom and to take over his family's seafood supply business when his father died. His mother passed away last year. And before you ask why I didn't tell you, Vash, you know why. You never wanted to hear any news regarding what was happening in Catalina Cove."

No, she hadn't, but anything having to do with K-Gee wasn't just town news. Bryce should have known that. "I'm sorry to hear about his parents. I really am. I'm surprised he's on the zoning board."

For years the townsfolk of the cove had never recognized members of the Pointe-au-Chien Native American tribe who lived on the east side of the bayou. Except for when it was time to pay city taxes. With K-Gee on the zoning board that meant change was possible in Catalina Cove after all.

"I need to know what you want to do, Vash," Bryce said, interrupting her thoughts. "The Barnes Group is giving us twenty days to finalize the deal or they will withdraw their offer."

Vashti stood up to cross the kitchen floor and put her teacup in the kitchen sink. "Okay, I'll think about what you said. Ten million dollars is a lot of money."

"Yes, and just think what you could do with it."

Vashti was thinking and she loved all the possibilities. Although she loved her job, she could stop working and spend the rest of her life traveling to

all those places her aunt always wanted to visit but
hadn't, because of putting Shelby by the Sea first.
Vashti wouldn't make the same mistake.

THE NEXT MORNING, for the first time in two years,
Vashti woke up feeling like she was in control of
her life and could finally see a light—a bright one
at that—at the end of the road. Scott was out of her
life, she had a great job, but more importantly, some
developer group was interested in her inn.

Her inn.

It seemed odd to think of Shelby by the Sea as
hers when it had belonged to her aunt for as long as
she could remember. Definitely long before Vashti
was born. Her parents' home had been a mile away,
and growing up she had spent a lot of her time at
Shelby; especially during her teen years when she
worked as her aunt's personal assistant. That's when
she'd fallen in love with the inn and had thought it
was the best place in the world.

Until…

Vashti pushed the "until" from her mind, refusing
to go there and hoping Bryce was wrong about her
having to return to Catalina Cove to face off with the
rezoning board. There had to be another way and she
intended to find it. Barely eighteen, she had needed
to escape the town that had always been her safe
haven because it had become a living hell for her.

An hour later Vashti had showered, dressed and
was walking out her door ready to start her day at
the Grand Nunes Luxury Hotel in Manhattan. But

not before stopping at her favorite café on the corner to grab a blueberry muffin and a cup of coffee. Catalina Cove was considered the blueberry capital in the country, and even she couldn't resist this small indulgence from her hometown. She would be the first to admit that although this blueberry muffin was delicious, it was not as good as the ones Bryce's mother made and sold at their family's restaurant.

With the bag containing her muffin in one hand and her cup of coffee in the other, Vashti caught the elevator up to the hotel's executive floor. She couldn't wait to get to work.

She'd heard that the big man himself, Gideon Nunes, was in town and would be meeting with several top members of the managerial and executive team, which would include her.

It was a half hour before lunch when she received a call to come to Mr. Nunes's office. Ten minutes later she walked out of the CEO's office stunned, in a state of shock. According to Mr. Nunes, his five hotels in the States had been sold, including this one. He'd further stated that the new owner was bringing in his own people, which meant her services were no longer needed.

In other words, she'd been fired.

CHAPTER TWO

A week later

VASHTI GLANCED AROUND the Louis Armstrong New Orleans International Airport. Although she'd never returned to Catalina Cove, she'd flown into this airport many times to attend a hotel conference or convention, or just to get away. Even though Catalina Cove was only an hour's drive away, she'd never been tempted to take the road trip to revisit the parish where she'd been born.

Today, with no job and more time on her hands than she really needed or wanted, in addition to the fact that there was ten million dollars dangling in front of her face, she was returning to Catalina Cove to attend the zoning board meeting and plead her case, although the thought of doing so was a bitter pill to swallow. When she'd left the cove she'd felt she didn't owe the town or its judgmental people anything. Likewise, they didn't owe her a thing. Now fourteen years later she was back and, to her way of thinking, Catalina Cove did owe her something.

Get 4 FREE REWARDS!

We'll send you 2 FREE Books plus 2 FREE Mystery Gifts.

Harlequin® Desire books feature heroes who have it all: wealth, status, incredible good looks... everything but the right woman.

FREE Value Over **$20**

SPECIAL EXCERPT FROM

HARLEQUIN®
Desire

*Scandal! The mayor's sister is marrying his nemesis!
Except it's just a rumor, and now the heiress needs
a real husband, fast. Enter her brother's sexy
best friend, security expert Emmett Keaton. It's the
perfect convenient marriage...until they can't keep
their hands to themselves!*

Read on for a sneak peek of
A Christmas Proposition *by Jessica Lemmon,
part of her* Dallas Billionaires Club *series!*

His eyes dipped briefly to her lips, igniting a sizzle in the air that had no place being there after he'd shared the sad story of his past. Even so, her answering reaction was to study his firm mouth in contemplation. The barely there scruff lining his angled jaw. His dominating presence made her feel fragile yet safe at the same time.

The urge to comfort him—to comfort herself—lingered. This time she didn't deny it.

With her free hand she reached up and cupped the thick column of his neck, tugging him down. He resisted, but only barely, stopping short a brief distance from her mouth to mutter one word.

"Hey…"

She didn't know if he'd meant to follow it with "this is a bad idea" or "we shouldn't get carried away," but she didn't wait to find out.

Her lips touched his gently and his mouth answered by puckering to return the kiss. Her eyes sank closed and his hand flinched against her palm.

He tasted…amazing. Like spiced cider and a capable, strong, heartbroken man who kept his hurts hidden from the outside world.

Eyes closed, she gripped the back of his neck tighter, angling her head to get more of his mouth. And when he pulled his hand from hers to come to rest on her shoulder, she swore she might melt from lust from that casual touch. His tongue came out to play, tangling with hers in a sensual, forbidden dance.

She used that free hand to fist his undershirt, tugging it up and brushing against the plane of his firm abs, and Emmett's response was to lift the hem of her sweater, where his rough fingertips touched the exposed skin of her torso.

A tight, needy sound escaped her throat, and his lips abruptly stopped moving against hers.

He pulled back, blinking at her with lust-heavy lids. She touched her mouth and looked away, the heady spell broken.

She'd just kissed her brother's best friend—a man who until today she might have jokingly described as her mortal enemy.

Worse, Emmett had kissed her back.

It was okay for this to be pretend—for their wedding to be an arrangement—but there was nothing black-and-white between them any longer. There was real attraction—as volatile as a live wire and as dangerous as a downed electric pole.

Whatever line they'd drawn by agreeing to marry, she'd stepped way, way over it.

He sobered quickly, recovering faster than she did. When he spoke, he echoed the words in her mind.

"That was a mistake."

Don't miss what happens next!
A Christmas Proposition *by Jessica Lemmon,*
part of her Dallas Billionaires Club series!

Available December 2018 wherever
Harlequin® Desire books and ebooks are sold.

www.Harlequin.com

HDEXP1118

Want to give in to temptation with
steamy tales of irresistible desire?

Check out **Harlequin® Presents®**,
Harlequin® Desire and
Harlequin® Kimani™ Romance books!

New books available every month!

CONNECT WITH US AT:

Facebook.com/groups/HarlequinConnection

 Facebook.com/HarlequinBooks

Twitter.com/HarlequinBooks

Instagram.com/HarlequinBooks

Pinterest.com/HarlequinBooks

ReaderService.com

(H)HARLEQUIN®

**ROMANCE WHEN
YOU NEED IT**

Love Harlequin romance?

DISCOVER.

Be the first to find out about promotions, news and exclusive content!

 Facebook.com/HarlequinBooks

 Twitter.com/HarlequinBooks

 Instagram.com/HarlequinBooks

 Pinterest.com/HarlequinBooks

ReaderService.com

EXPLORE.

Sign up for the Harlequin e-newsletter and download a free book from any series at **TryHarlequin.com.**

CONNECT.

Join our Harlequin community to share your thoughts and connect with other romance readers!
Facebook.com/groups/HarlequinConnection

**ROMANCE WHEN
YOU NEED IT**

HSOCIAL2018

Reward the book lover in you!

Earn points on your purchase of new Harlequin books from participating retailers.

Turn your points into **FREE BOOKS** of your choice!

Join for FREE today at
www.HarlequinMyRewards.com.

Harlequin My Rewards is a free program (no fees) without any commitments or obligations.